The Library at Warwick School
Please return or renew on or before the last date below

4/15

4/12/15

0 4 DEC 2015

2 4 JUN 2016

D0542319

ALSO BY BENJAMIN ZEPHANIAH

Face
Refugee Boy
Gangsta Rap
Teacher's Dead

Benjamin Zephaniah

Terror Kid

HOT
KEY
BOOKS

First published in Great Britain in 2014 by Hot Key Books
Northburgh House, 10 Northburgh Street, London EC1V 0AT

Copyright © Benjamin Zephaniah 2014

The moral rights of the author have been asserted.

All rights reserved.
No part of this publication may be reproduced, stored or transmitted
in any form by any means, electronic, mechanical, photocopying or
otherwise, without the prior written permission of the publisher.

All characters in this publication are fictitious and any resemblance to
real persons, living or dead, is purely coincidental.

A CIP catalogue record for this book is available from the British
Library.

ISBN: 978-1-4714-0177-0

2

This book is typeset in 10.5 Berling LT Std using Atomik ePublisher

Printed and bound by Clays Ltd, St Ives Plc

www.hotkeybooks.com

Hot Key Books is part of the Bonnier Publishing Group
www.bonnierpublishing.com

For the kids of Broadway Comprehensive School,
the kids of Birmingham who try their best,
and Tony Benn (RIP), who first told me to
write this book.

Chapter 1

Riot in Progress

Rico stood and stared as the shopping trolley flew through the air and smashed through the sports shop window. The boots and shoulders of the rioters had already weakened the toughened glass, and the force of the trolley caused the whole pane to shatter and collapse. Before the glass had even settled, a sea of people charged into the shop. The rioters danced, they chanted and they celebrated as they left the shop carrying balls, bats, trainers and football shirts, anything they could pick up and carry away.

It was a hot, sticky Friday night in Birmingham, but the riots happening there had started five days earlier when a young woman had been shot dead by police in Leyton, East London. Young people all over London were angered, and started protests and demonstrations. On one of those demonstrations a police officer pushed another teenage girl to the ground and kicked her whilst she was down. A bystander filmed it all on his phone and uploaded it to the Internet, and then the anger spread. The demonstrations turned to riots, and in a few days the riots had spread west to Bristol and north to Wolverhampton, Salford, Nottingham, Manchester and Rico's city, Birmingham. The British people, mainly young people of all races, all faiths, and many with no faith, were rioting up and down the country. They had had enough.

Rico Federico stood on Dudley Road and watched as shop after shop was smashed, rushed and then emptied. A large number of police wearing hard helmets and dressed in heavy black protective clothing gathered at the top of the road carrying shields. The police charged but they were outnumbered by the mob and were soon forced back to watch from their lines. A police car and a bus were set on fire. Fire alarms, car alarms and burglar alarms rang out from near and far, and Rico seemed to be the only one standing still. He turned a full circle to see the destruction all about him. Suddenly someone put their arm around his shoulders and ran their fingers through his hair.

'Rico, it's showtime,' a voice shouted in his ear.

It was Karima. Karima was the tough, fiery daughter of Somalian refugees and the closest Rico had to a best friend, but they were very different in character. Karima was charismatic and had many other friends. Rico just had Karima. She was into kick-boxing and grappling; Rico couldn't beat a doll up. Karima was loud, cool and streetwise; Rico wasn't. Karima was addicted to social networking sites; Rico didn't care for them. But even though Rico wasn't interested in chatting to people online or collecting hundreds of online friends, he was definitely into computer hardware, computer programming and his computer repair business. He was really into computers. But to relax they both loved playing computer games. Karima just loved the thrill of winning, whilst Rico would spend time modifying the code and changing the graphics. They were an odd couple.

Rico was surprised to see her.

'What you doing here?' said Rico, looking at the gang of other people that she was with.

'Shopping, man,' she said with a wide grin on her face.

'Shopping?' Rico replied disapprovingly.

'The revolution has come, let's go shopping!' Karima shouted, beckoning him on as if into battle.

'It doesn't work like that,' said Rico, taking her arm off his shoulder.

Karima and her gang ran off into a phone shop to continue their shopping, and Rico began to walk away.

Everybody, it seemed, was doing something, either heading to a shop to get free stuff, or leaving a shop with their hands full. Some carried their loot on top of their heads, some on bicycles, and others used shopping trolleys from the very shops they had looted. It was so easy. The police were at one end of the street, but the rest of the street belonged to the looters, who just took what they wanted and left at the other end. As he walked away Rico heard his name being called behind him. It was Karima and her gang. They ran past him with their hands full of boxes and bags.

'See you later, brov,' shouted Karima as they ran off triumphantly.

Rico carried on walking up Dudley Road and before long he had left the rioting behind and reached the road where he lived. As he turned the corner a police van screeched to a stop. Four officers jumped out of the van and ran up to him, but Rico wasn't worried, he was calm and ready to explain that he had nothing to do with the riots. But there was no time for that; he was taken straight to the ground before he could say a word.

'Where's the stuff you took?' asked one officer.

'I didn't take any stuff.' Rico's face was being pushed into the ground, his lips pressed against the pavement, making it difficult to speak.

'You're under arrest for theft!' yelled the officer.

'But I haven't taken anything!' shouted Rico as he was picked up and thrown into the cage at the back of the van. The van door was slammed shut. Rico was alone, and there was silence. Then the van drove off at high speed. It wasn't the first time that Rico had been picked up by the police for no reason. Rico could only think about his parents and the stress his arrest would cause them. They had worked so hard to get where they were now. Both his parents were Spanish Romany. As children in Spain, his parents had been spat at, beaten up and refused education. But they had been determined to make a new life for themselves. They came to Birmingham where his father had worked as a builder and then started a small building firm of his own. It was doing well but then they decided to have a family. Then he got work in the city planning department. He was quickly promoted so his rise from nomad to city planner was fast. His mother started her new life in England sewing shirts in a sweatshop, and then she went to college, studied hard, did her training, and became a nurse.

Rico's parents had often taken him to the library as a young boy and as he grew older he had read about the history of the Romany people. But he didn't identify himself as Romany, He was a Brummie; born and bred in Birmingham, with a Birmingham accent. With his straight nose, light skin and mousy hair, no one would guess he had Romany roots, not even other Roma people. He didn't smile much, he didn't hang out in gangs, he didn't follow the crowd, and he didn't care what people thought of him. Friends came and went, but that didn't worry him. He didn't use the word 'politics' much – like his parents, he didn't care for political parties, but he did care about people. In the library and inspired by his parents' lives he had searched out stories of how other people struggled and fought for their rights and of how sometimes people's rights were taken away from them. Like millions of other people he watched the news on television and saw wars and famines around the world, he saw how people were forced to flee their countries for safety, and how one group of people could oppress another, and when he had listened to all the politicians talking and making excuses, he still couldn't understand why. Why people did the things they did to each other, and why decent people didn't rise up to end the conflicts and inequalities in the world. He was sensitive to the suffering of others, but just feeling sorry for them was not enough: he wanted to help them, he wanted to do something. He was angry, but his anger was silent. He hated violence, but he wanted to change the world. He just didn't know how.

Chapter 2

Fire in Progress

The police van arrived at the station, and Rico was taken by two officers to the front desk. It was a busy night. Rico was waiting for the Enquiry Officer to process two people in front of him when he heard a commotion outside. He could hear officers shouting, telling their captives to be quiet, but they got louder and louder as they got nearer. Rico kept looking ahead until they entered the station and he heard his name.

'Rico. What's happening, bad boy?' It was Karima. She was grinning as if nothing was wrong.

'What kind of a question is that?' said Rico. 'Can't you see they've arrested me?'

'So what stuff did you get?'

'Nothing. You know I was just walking home and minding my own business,' Rico replied.

'You see,' said Karima, pointing to Rico as if he was a naughty boy. 'You should have done some shopping, brov, at least you would have done something to get arrested for.'

The others, three boys and one girl, all began to laugh, but Rico, not wanting to engage with any of them, just turned away and looked at the back of the boy in front of him.

'They're laughing, but even you know this isn't funny,' said Rico.

One of the many arresting officers now standing in the reception area shouted, 'Right, that's enough. Keep your noise down.'

Karima and her friends continued to laugh and snigger, ignoring the seriousness of their situation. Karima, as usual, was the leader of the pack and did most of the talking, working hard at giving the impression she was having fun. Rico always thought that Karima overdosed on fun to overcome the pain of her childhood. She had seen too much brutality of war in her homeland. But Rico didn't do fun. Outside of his family, Rico just couldn't find much fun in the world to be joyous about.

The Enquiry Officer at the front desk checked them in and they were all formally arrested, then they were separated and led away for questioning. Rico was taken to a room where he was told to sit down by the officer who had arrested him. The officer sat opposite him but said nothing for a couple of minutes. When he did speak he did so quietly, and slowly.

'Right, young man, listen to me carefully. My name is Detective Constable Holland. I'm going to give you a few more moments to think about where you are, and then I want you to tell me who called you out onto the streets tonight, and where you hid the goods that you stole.'

Rico wasn't playing his game.

'I don't need any more moments. I don't need anything from you. What I need is to go home, because no one called me out, I didn't steal anything, and you got nothing on me.'

'We got something on you all right,' said the officer, maintaining his low, serious tone.

'What?' asked Rico.

'We saw you walking down Dudley Road, we

saw you talking to your criminally minded friends, and we know that you entered at least one shop on the Dudley Road and helped yourself to some stock. My colleagues are looking at CCTV footage as we speak, so soon, if you can't remember, I'll be able to show you what you've been up to. So you might as well tell me now. That way we save time and get this stuff done with quickly.'

Rico cracked a small smile. 'It's all good then. I can't wait to see this footage.'

'Good,' said the officer. 'I suppose you're now going to demand a lawyer and you're going to tell me that I should respect your human rights.' He pointed to the door. 'Well, what about the human rights of the people you're robbing out there? Hey, what about them?'

Rico was unmoved. 'I don't need a lawyer, and I ain't said anything about my human rights. I just want to see this footage you have of me.'

Another officer put his head around the door; Officer Holland saw him, and said, 'I'll be back.' And left the room.

Rico sat looking around the pale, empty walls for five minutes, then Detective Constable Holland returned and opened the door as wide as it could go.

'Right, pick yourself up, you're free to go.' He seemed to speak reluctantly, acting as if the conversation they'd just had hadn't happened.

Rico slapped the table and spoke angrily.

'You see. I'm sick of this. So where's this footage of me? There isn't any, is there? No, you lot just lost control of the streets, so you just start picking up everyone you can to make up for your stupidity.'

The officer stared angrily at Rico. 'What's this? You want to stay, do you? I'm sure it can be arranged.'

'I'm sure it can be arranged too, but whatever you lot do you can't scare me. Stop and search me as much as you like, arrest me as much as you like, you don't scare me,' said Rico. 'Give me my stuff and let me go. I don't need to stay here any longer.'

Rico stood up and followed the officer out to the reception. As they arrived Rico saw his father confronting the desk sergeant. His father was short, but he made the noise of many men as he stamped his feet, banged his fist on the desk, and pointed with his other hand, shouting at the sergeant.

'Let me in. I want to see my son now. You have no right to keep him here.'

The desk sergeant shuffled some papers around and replied without looking up.

'I told you, sir, we're bringing him out to you. Raising your voice will not speed up the process.'

'Process. What process? You don't have any process, you're just a bunch of crooks and liars. And don't call me sir. Now, where is he?'

'Here I am,' said Rico.

'Over to you, Sarge,' said the officer.

Rico's father, Stefan, shouted, 'Rico. Have they charged you?'

'No. They can't touch me,' Rico replied.

'You haven't heard the last of this,' said Stefan to the desk sergeant. 'I'm going to lodge a complaint.'

'You're free to do so,' said the desk sergeant, who then waved Rico over. 'I need you to sign for your possessions and you can be off.'

Rico's father carried on at the desk sergeant.

'You think you can do whatever you like? Well, you can't. This is the fifth time you've picked him up this year, for no reason at all. He's fifteen, what do you want to do, give him a criminal record before he's sixteen? You haven't heard the last of this. You wait. This isn't the end.'

Handing over a see-through polythene bag with

Rico's belongings, the sergeant said, 'He was just in the wrong place at the wrong time.'

'The wrong place at the wrong time?' shouted Stefan, his voice getting even louder as he repeated the sergeant's words. 'The wrong place at the wrong time? That's what you lot say every time you pick him up. The wrong place at the wrong time. He was born in this area, he lives in this area, he goes to school in this area, and he keeps getting picked up in this area. So now you tell me, where is the right place at the right time? Come on, tell me.'

'Come on, Dad, let's go,' said Rico.

Rico and his father left the station and began to walk home. The air was thick with smoke, the streets were busy, sirens could be heard all around, and tension marked every face. As they got to the bottom of the road a car screeched round the corner and sped towards the station. Rico and his father turned to look. The car came to a sudden stop. Two arms appeared out of the side windows, both holding lit petrol bombs, which they threw at the police station. One hit the police station sign, and the other landed in the doorway. The car sped away, going from nought to sixty in six seconds, and

Rico watched as the flames got bigger. The steps to the police station were ablaze, flames began to cover the door, police officers ran out spraying foam from fire extinguishers. Rico turned and began to head towards the station. 'We have to help them, Dad,' Rico said.

His father grabbed his arm and pulled him back.

'No, Rico,' he said. 'They're taking care of it themselves. It's got nothing to do with us. We're just in the wrong place, at the wrong time.'

Chapter 3

Computer Kid

At home Rico apologised to his father for disturbing his night, but Stefan laughed and began to tell stories of the many times that his own father had had to get him out of police stations. Rico listened, but his mind was somewhere else.

'I wonder what happened at the station after we left,' he said.

'They would have dealt with it,' replied his father. 'They have the equipment and all the right contacts.'

'I really hope no one got hurt.'

'So do I. But let me tell you something, you're worrying about them a lot more than they're worrying about you.'

Rico went up to his room to work on his computers. He had begun writing software for games when he was twelve. He read everything he could about computers, the people behind computers, the writing of software and the future of computers. It was his passion. His first computer had been a cheap laptop that he had bought from a second-hand shop but even after he had upgraded it, it was too slow for what he needed to do, so he passed it on to his mother. He had a Saturday job at Telford's PC, a computer shop in the city centre. The shop sold computers and accessories, but because of his knowledge Rico was allowed to pursue a sideline in computer repairs. This helped bring customers into the shop, and earned extra for him. The owner, Timothy Telford, had another employee called Ana. Rico liked Ana. She was obsessed with dressmaking and every day she came to work she would be showing off one of her creations. She worked hard in the computer shop, but her ambition was to earn enough money to start her own business making and selling dresses.

When Rico was given toys as a small boy he didn't play with them, he took them apart. He would check every detail, examine every single part, observe how they worked, and then put them back together. He felt that he couldn't play with them if he didn't know how they worked. From toy cars to tricycles, from torches to radios, he explored them all, and now he had progressed to computers.

Rico's repair business was flourishing. As well as the customers that came into the shop, there were always friends, and friends of friends, who would turn up at his house with broken games, tablets and laptops. In his bedroom he had three fully networked desktop computers, which he had made from recycled parts he got from friends, or leftover parts he got from the shop. Now he was building another computer.

He had two tables covered with computer equipment. His latest creation was on a table by the window. He had only been working on it for two days but it was to be his most powerful yet. The keyboard and monitor were in place waiting to be connected to a main case, with a fan, a sound card and a couple of memory sticks. Most of these parts had been liberated from a box of so-called junk that an estate agent had thrown out.

Rico loved history, but he knew the future was in computers.

Chapter 4

More Work, Less Pay

City Hospital was busy. Rico's mother, Lena, spent most of her shift tending to the elderly patients on her ward. Lena had worked on this ward for two years and she had also worked on the children's ward, the emergency ward and the maternity ward in her time, so she was very experienced.

City Hospital was on Dudley Road, so some of the hospital staff could hear the riots as they were happening on the streets. Lena was asked to go and help in the emergency department – she had the experience, and they were desperate. She arrived to find nurses and doctors rushing around, frantically trying to keep up with all the casualties coming in.

The Accident and Emergency ward was always busy, but tonight was like no other. Along with the DIY casualties and the drink- and-drug abusers, there were those who had been touched by the riots. Most of these casualties were people who had fallen or been pushed over as the crowds took to the streets, some were victims of robberies, and others were shopkeepers who had tried to defend their businesses.

Lena was thanked for working her many extra hours and told that she was free to go. She went to the hospital car park, got into her old, battered car and drove home.

As soon as Lena entered her house Rico came down from his room to see her, and as soon as she saw him she called him over.

'Come here and give me a hug,' she said, her arms out wide.

As they were hugging, Stefan came into the living room and launched into the story of Rico's latest arrest. Lena wasn't surprised – he had already been stopped many times that year – but she was relieved to know that he had been released and not injured in the riots. Lena listened and when Stefan had told his story she began hers.

'Well, what about my day at the office? There I was, happily tending to my little old ladies, when suddenly I'm asked to go to A&E to deal with a great big policeman who tells me that some kids beat him up, and then I have to deal with a fifteen-year-old boy who tells me that he had been kicked and beaten with a truncheon by a policeman. I used to work in the NHS, now I work in a war zone. And last week they told us that we have a pay freeze for another year. They keep giving us more targets to reach with fewer staff and less money.'

Rico saw how tired and frustrated his mum looked.

She threw her bag down on the sofa. 'I guess you expect me to make dinner now?'

'No way,' said Stefan. 'I've been slaving in that kitchen for the last hour preparing something just for you. And you,' he said to Rico.

'Now, let me guess,' said Lena. 'Pasta.'

'How did you know?' asked Stefan.

'Well, every time you cook up a surprise, it's pasta,' said Lena. 'Don't you get it? That means it's not a surprise any more.'

'It's pasta,' Stefan said, grinning. 'But not as you know it. It's pasta with a twist.'

'Oh, yes. What's the twist?

'Salad,' replied Stefan, throwing his hands up as if completing a magic trick.

'It will do – again!' said Lena. Her face was tired but she was smiling.

'Maybe I'll just go for the salad,' said Rico. 'The last time I had your pasta it stayed around for days.'

'You said you liked it,' said Stefan.

'I was just trying to encourage you,' replied Rico. 'I realise now it was a mistake.'

Stefan stamped his foot down as if to chase Rico, but he was laughing. 'Get out of here.'

Rico ran upstairs to check on his computer work and Lena went to change her clothes.

Rico's software had downloaded, but his mother's words were still running around his head, so he left his work and started to look at news reports about the health service and the targets they had to reach. Then he began looking at all the cuts the service was suffering, and in a chat room for health service workers he read their own stories of depression and hardship. Very soon he was on the local National Health Service site. He looked around it for a time and soon he found a login area for administrators. Rico became curious, so using the password-cracking software he had developed to help people who had forgotten their own passwords, within a few minutes he managed to gain access to the back end of the site, and found details and login credentials of other systems within the NHS. He entered the payroll system and keyed in his mother's name. He could see her years of service, her position in the hospital, her National Insurance number and her wages. Then he saw in bold red letters: TRADE UNION ACTIVIST.

Stefan shouted up from the bottom of the stairs, 'Your dinner's ready.' Rico quickly closed his mother's profile and loaded some more software that would help hide any trace of his activities.

Downstairs, the family sat down to eat and, after an initial tasting of the food, both Lena and Rico gave it the thumbs up.

'This is quite nice, you know,' said Lena.

'Yes,' said Rico. 'I really like it.'

'You see,' said Stefan. 'I told you it was different.'

'Something's happening in this country,' said Lena. 'Accident and Emergency used to be full of men falling off ladders, children falling off swings, and women falling off their heels. Now it's stab wounds and bullet holes, and tonight it's revolution.'

'I wish it was revolution,' said Stefan.

'I wish they'd all just go home. Nothing's going to change by smashing up a few shops,' said Rico.

'How come you're so sensible?' said Lena. 'You didn't get it from your dad. Anyway, are you OK?'

'I'm fine,' replied Rico.

'How did they treat you?'

'Like they always do,' said Rico.

'You didn't do anything, did you?'

Rico was surprised by her question. 'Mum, come on. You know I'm not doing anything wrong out there.'

'I'm sorry.'

Stefan interrupted. 'Wrong place, wrong time again.'

'When is it not the wrong place, and the wrong time?' Lena sighed, leaning over and stroking Rico's arm.

'That's exactly what I said,' said Stefan. 'That's exactly what I said.'

Rico ate his food as quickly as he could and stood up from the table.

'Excuse me. I've got to go. I've got some software running that I need to check.'

As Rico was heading back upstairs his mother asked, 'So how are your computers then?'

'It's all good,' Rico replied. 'I got four now.'

Lena thought he was exaggerating. 'Rico! Two days ago you told me you had three and you were going to start work on another one.'

'That's right,' Rico said casually. 'I was building another one, and now I've finished it.'

'You finished it already?'

'Yes, I told you I would get it done before the end of the week.'

'And I heard you, but I thought you were talking about next week. What are you doing with four of them?' she asked. 'Are you now going to start selling them as well as fixing them?'

'I don't know. I might do.' Rico replied. 'I just like building them and writing software. To test some of the codes I've written I needed a network of computers, so I've created my own network.'

Lena looked at Stefan proudly and said, 'He's so clever. Didn't we do well?'

'Got to go,' said Rico, slightly embarrassed. 'I left

my computers working on something in parallel and I need to check the output.'

'I need to check on you too,' shouted Lena. 'Parental guidance. I know what you teenagers are like.'

Chapter 5

States of Emergency

Some were calling it the summer of discontent. And it was not just in Britain. A series of uprisings had begun in Tunisia and spread to Egypt, Bahrain, Saudi Arabia, Morocco and other Arab and North African countries. Russia demanded free and fair elections. Then the uprisings started in Europe. Hungarians took to the streets so their voices could be heard. Portugal, Spain and Italy were running out of money, and in Greece there were daily riots as workers demanded better wages and pensions, and the unemployed demanded jobs.

Britain was broke, and the government raised taxes on fuel and goods in shops. Household taxes were raised too, but as homelessness increased, cuts were made to the money spent on charities, youth clubs, art centres, services for the disabled, libraries and schools, whilst at the same time the fees that university students had to pay were raised. So as unemployment rose, people took to the streets. Those who were educated, connected and organised began to plan marches and demonstrations. Those who were not, simply went out and vented their anger on the streets in any way they could. Sometimes that meant occupying banks and churches, sometimes it meant burning and looting.

In the weeks and months following the riots in Britain, the government ordered the courts to open late into the night and at weekends. They requested that, where possible, judges give out maximum sentences to make examples of the offenders, and to administer judgement swiftly. Tired judges and lawyers struggled to keep up with the numbers of young people being taken into custody, and most newspaper reports failed to question why such riots would happen in the first place, simply portraying all the rioters as mindless thugs.

Karima and her friends were treated leniently because of their age. They were sentenced to one month in youth custody. They were warned that any appearance in front of the courts in the future would attract much longer sentences. They were lucky. One fourteen-year-old was sentenced to four years for sending a text message to his friends telling them to take to the streets. His friends didn't take to the streets, and nor did he, but the judge said: 'It's the thought that counts.'

Rico was angry. He watched what was happening around the world, frustrated that he couldn't do anything about it. He watched television programmes about how the rich lived and how the poor lived, and how people lived divided all over the planet. Everything he saw made him realise that people all over the world could have much better lives if they had more of a say in the way their lives were governed. He believed in the power of the people. His problem was, he just didn't know many people. He didn't know anybody like him: people who weren't rioting but who wanted to do something. He had nowhere to go to find like-minded people. He had tried to start debating groups at school but there had been no interest. He had tried to organise a group of kids at school to go on a demonstration supporting his mother and her trade union when they were on strike, but no one turned up. He went on his own to demonstrations organised by university students who were protesting about the rise in their fees. The first student protest he went on was with his sister when she was a student, but he felt so strongly about issues concerning young people that even when Lola had left home he went on other demonstrations. On these demonstrations he would not chant or sing, he would just walk silently. He just wanted to be counted.

Chapter 6

More Work, More Pay

The day after the riots, Rico went to work as he always did. There were still small pockets of unrest and there were noticeably fewer people around than usual, so business in the shop was slow. The newspapers, the television and the Internet were covering news of the troubles. Students from all over the West Midlands were going to march through the city centre protesting against increases in university fees. The police had told them not to, but the student union insisted that the march would go ahead. It had been planned months in advance, and they were not going to reschedule. Rico wanted to go on that march and, just like the student union, he'd be stopped by nothing. He had to show his solidarity. He knew the issues, and he wasn't going to wait until he was a student before he started caring.

With so few customers visiting the shop, Rico was allowed to leave work early. He walked the short distance to Digbeth, where the students and their supporters had gathered. After some speeches and a lecture from the stewards on how to behave, they began walking towards the city centre. After an hour Rico was beginning to wish that he had brought something to eat. He was getting hungrier and hungrier, but they kept marching on, and the more they marched the louder they became. Rico started to get tired, but he was encouraged by the demonstrators chanting, the drummers drumming out rhythms to match their chants, people blowing whistles, and onlookers shouting words of support. But he was still hungry.

The sun began to get brighter and hotter, and by the time they reached Colmore Circus their numbers had swelled and spirits were high. The crowd gathered in front of a large stage to hear speeches from student leaders, trade unionists and poets. As he stood listening to a student reading her poem, Rico heard someone call his name.

'Rico.'

The voice came from close behind him, so close he thought it might have been in his head. Then he heard it again.

'Rico. How's it going, mate?'

This time Rico looked behind him and saw a tall man smiling at him. Rico ignored him; if this wasn't the man who had called his name, Rico didn't want to embarrass himself. After all, the man smiling could just be smiling because he was happy, or because he liked the poem. Rico just wasn't sure, so he turned back and continued listening to the poet.

'Rico. I'm your man,' the voice said again.

This time when Rico turned around, the man spoke to him directly.

'Good to see you.'

The man moved so that he was directly in front of Rico.

'It's a good turnout.'

'It's all right,' replied Rico.

The man was in his late thirties, clean-shaven and smartly dressed in pressed trousers, white shirt and black waistcoat. Despite his well-ironed image there was something edgy about him. He had two small earrings in each ear, and a tattoo of a lion's head on his neck. He continued to look ahead as he spoke.

'Students love to demonstrate – they always have done – but what happens when they grow up?'

'So what are you saying?' said Rico. 'Don't you support them?'

'Yeah, of course I support them, otherwise I wouldn't be here. I just wonder where it's leading, what it changes.'

'So do I,' Rico said. 'But it's better than doing nothing. Who are you, anyway, and how do you know my name?'

'You just don't know who to trust nowadays.'

'What does that mean?'

The man looked at Rico, and then he looked into the distance.

'I support the students, but I came here to see you. Can we go somewhere to talk?'

'I'm not going anywhere with you. I don't know you from Adam.'

'You didn't know me, but you do now,' the man said, smiling. 'My name's Speech.'

'What kind of a name is that? And just knowing your name is not knowing you.'

'Put it like this, everyone calls me Speech.'

Rico frowned. 'How do you know my name, anyway?'

'I make it my business to know stuff, and we have a friend in common. Don't worry, it's all cool.'

Rico was beginning to get angry.

'Stop talking rubbish, man, and tell me about this friend and tell me what you want.'

Speech dropped his voice in an attempt to sound friendlier.

'Come on, let's go for a walk.'

Rico's anger heightened.

'What's wrong with you, guy? I told you, I'm not going anywhere with you, I don't know you, man.'

'It's all cool,' said Speech. 'Just give me a few minutes for a quick chat. I want to put some work your way.'

'If you want to put work my way you come to the shop. I'm there every Saturday. If not, just leave your computer and the staff will make a note of what you want me to do.'

'No, I can't do that. Come on. Let's walk. I'll explain why.'

Rico looked around as he thought about walking

away. As he caught Speech's eye, Speech cracked a smile.

'Trust me,' said Speech. 'It's a job, a good job. If you don't want it, don't take it – but at least hear me out.'

'OK. But that's all I'm doing. Hearing you out,' replied Rico nervously.

They began to move away from the demonstration, but Speech dictated the route, and as they walked Speech made small talk about the weather, the rising price of music downloads, and the lack of good music in the charts. Rico kept looking around trying to see if there was anyone else involved, others who might be watching and waiting, but he saw nothing that looked suspicious. After a bit more small talk, he didn't feel he was in any danger, but he couldn't think what Speech would want with him.

They came to a large road junction and went down a subway to pass underneath. At the centre of the subway system was a plot of grass with a water feature that wasn't working. Speech stopped. Rico stopped.

'So, what's up?' asked Rico.

'Like I said, I need you to do some work for me.'

'Repairs depend on the price of parts, but if you want me to write a programme for you it's £100 a day, paid at the end of each day, in cash. For half days, £50 – anything over a half costs you full.'

Speech nodded approvingly. 'You could be a businessman.'

'I am a businessman,' said Rico.

'Could you build a website for me?'

'Of course I can.'

'How long will it take you?'

'It depends on how big you want it.'

'Just an average-size website, but I want it custom built. Not one of these cheap off-the-shelf ones. I want good graphics, sharp photos, and it's got to be user-friendly.'

Rico thought for a while. He didn't get jobs like these often, but when he did they earned him good money, and he needed some extra money for his future business plans.

'An average-size, custom-built website, made from scratch, with you providing all the photos and links, will take me about two weeks. That will cost you £1400.'

Rico thought it sounded expensive and Speech

would start talking the price down. He waited for him to start bargaining, but he didn't.

'Cool. I'll give you £2000.'

'Are you listening to me, man? I said it would cost you £1400.'

'I know,' said Speech. 'But I want to pay you two grand.'

Rico was taken aback. 'What the hell do you want to pay me two thousand for? I only asked for one thousand, four hundred. Are you crazy or what?'

'I told you we had a friend in common.'

'Yes. Who is it?'

'Ana.'

'Who? Ana that works in the shop?'

'Yes, that Ana. You know what she does for a hobby?'

'Yes, she designs and makes dresses.'

'That's right. I'm a good friend of hers. She did a big favour for me once, and I want to repay her by getting this website built for her. But you have to keep it a secret. It's really important. This must be kept a secret until her birthday. Don't mention it to her. I want this to be the best birthday present she's ever had. Do you see what I'm trying to do?'

'I see,' said Rico. 'So that's why you can't come into the shop?'

'That's right. And that's why I'm paying you extra. This has to be between me and you.'

Speech went into his inside jacket pocket and took out an envelope. He held it out as he spoke. 'Here are two memory sticks with photos and text on them. I'm leaving it up to you to design it. You need to have a shop area so people can buy online; all the prices are there so you can build a checkout area and all that stuff. You'll see the name of her company – you need to use that and buy her a domain name.'

'In that case I'll need a deposit,' said Rico.

'There's also £2000 in this envelope. That's all your money, and more, up front.'

'You don't need to do that,' Rico said.

'I know I don't, but I want to. I want to leave you to it. I trust you, so I want you to use your initiative, do what you think is good.'

'Shall I call you?' asked Rico.

'No, I don't have a phone. I'll find you, don't worry about that, just go and do the job – but remember, not a word.'

He handed Rico the envelope. Rico could feel the

memory sticks and the thickness of the banknotes. 'I'll start straight away,' he said.

Speech said goodbye and walked away, leaving Rico still thinking about the unusual deal he had just done.

Chapter 7

Woodpecker Remembered

Rico got to work on the website straight away. He didn't tell anyone about his new job. He had built websites before, mainly for his friends' bands, but he had never built one this big, and he'd never done one for this much money. He was determined to make a good job of it. On one of the memory sticks he found all the text that was promoting the business, and on the other he found photos of dresses with descriptions and prices. He had been paid well, and because he had been given creative freedom he planned to try out as many of his new ideas as possible.

He still did a bit of work for people who needed

small jobs done, but he used all the time he could to work on the website. After a week he had to go back to do his day in the computer shop, where he was very tempted to ask Ana questions. He wasn't tempted to actually tell her about the website – he really liked the idea of surprising her on her birthday – but he was tempted to ask her what her favourite colour was, to make that the dominant colour on her home page, or what her favourite type of music was, so he could incorporate some on the site, or if she had a business logo in mind, but he didn't, just in case she got suspicious. At the end of the day he left the shop and was making his way to the bus stop when Speech just appeared, walking alongside him. Rico was startled but tried not to show it and kept walking as if nothing had happened.

'How's it going?' asked Speech.

'It's all good,' replied Rico.

'How's the website?'

'Like I said, it's all good.'

'That's what I like to hear.'

'Do you want to see it? You can if you like,' said Rico.

'No, I just wanted to see if there was anything you needed.'

'I don't need anything. I'm almost there.'

Suddenly Speech stopped. Rico carried on talking.

'There's a couple of things I'd like to know from Ana, but they're not that important, I can fix them later.'

'So you haven't said anything to her then?' asked Speech.

Rico came back quickly. 'Of course not. I said I wouldn't.'

'She's a good woman,' said Speech. 'She deserves the best. Don't you think so?'

'Of course, that's why I'm going to make a wicked site for her,' said Rico. 'Keep walking. I got a bus to catch. Work to do.'

'No. This is as far as I go. So everything's all right then?'

'Yes, everything's all right,' said Rico, now a little tired of the questions.

'Great. I'll see you soon.'

Speech turned and walked away in the opposite direction.

On the bus Rico sat comfortably at the back on the top deck. His phone rang. It was his mother asking if he was on his way home. Rico told her that he would be back soon. He folded his arms, leaned against the window and began to doze. He was very tired, but he wasn't worried he would miss his stop: he had dozed many times on this route and because he knew the route so well he always woke up just before his stop. He started to think about Karima. He was upset with her behaviour in the riots, but he was missing her. He made up his mind that he would go to her house to find out where she was being held, and then visit her. Then he began to think about his sister, Lola. He was still able to hear the sound of the bus and the passengers around him, but he was relaxed enough to drift into a dreamlike state, recalling happy memories of his big sister playing with him in their garden or the local park. When she was small, Lola had liked to carve shapes into trees using sharp stones, so Rico had given her the nickname Woodpecker. He recalled the time she had spent teaching him how to ride his bicycle, and how when they were older Lola would tell him stories of how good overcomes evil.

Rico was very close to his sister, but his parents didn't talk to him about why she had left home so suddenly. He really missed her.

Rico jumped up just before the bus reached his stop. He ran down the stairs, off the bus, and didn't stop running until he reached his home, where his dinner was on the table. Rico wanted to take his plate and go up to his room, but his mother wasn't having it.

'No,' she said. 'We've hardly seen you lately, up there on your computers. They can wait. Sit down and eat.'

'OK,' said Rico.

The atmosphere during the meal was upbeat and happy, with Lena doing most of the talking. She was always full of stories about characters that she encountered at the hospital. All was going well until Rico brought up the subject that was really on his mind.

'Have you heard from Lola?'

There was an awkward silence at the table. Stefan spoke first.

'If she'd got in contact with us, we would have told you, wouldn't we?'

Lena continued. 'We were wondering if she'd been in contact with you.'

'I told you before,' said Rico. 'I haven't got her number.'

'And nor have we,' said Lena. 'She calls sometimes, but unless she contacts one of us, we can't contact her. It's as simple as that.'

'Don't you want to talk to her?' asked Rico.

Lena dropped her knife and fork onto her plate in anger.

'Of course we want to talk to her. She left us, we didn't kick her out. You still have this idea that we're the bad people, but she's the one who decided to go, and she's the one who's decided not to stay in contact. So don't blame us, Rico.'

'I'm not blaming you,' said Rico softly.

'Good,' said Lena.

'OK. Enjoy your meal,' said Stefan.

Rico continued to eat, but he didn't enjoy his meal.

Chapter 8

Friends Reunited?

Rico had been working late into the night, so when he was woken early in the morning by the noise his parents were making getting up, he tried to ignore them. They were leaving for their weekly shop at the supermarket. He listened as the car drove away and then he curled up to try to sleep some more. He tried, but he couldn't. He was physically tired, but his mind began working overtime. He worked best at night, and he was planning to work hard that night too, so he needed the night more than he needed the day. He kept telling himself to go to sleep, but the more he told himself, the harder it was to sleep. He eventually began to drift off, but then his phone rang. He reached over, and picked it up, putting the phone to his ear without opening his eyes.

'Hello. Who is it?' he groaned.

The voice on the phone was upbeat and wide awake.

'What's going on, brov? Long time.'

It was Karima. Rico was surprised to hear her.

'Where are you? he asked.

'I'm out.'

'You're out already?' Rico said. 'I was thinking of coming to see you but I've been busy, and I didn't know where you were.'

'Don't worry about it. Just done a few weeks. Good behaviour, you know what I'm saying?'

'I know what you're saying, but I don't believe you.'

'What do you mean, you don't believe me?' asked Karima.

'You can't do good behaviour,' Rico replied.

Karima laughed. 'I can, you know – well, I can make people believe I'm doing good behaviour. Anyway, I'm out now and I wanna see you. Important stuff, you get me?'

'No problem,' said Rico. 'Give me a call tomorrow

or something. Come round in the afternoon, maybe.'

'Tomorrow! I'm talking about today, brov. What you doing now?'

'I'm in bed.'

'Get up. I'm coming now.'

Rico groaned. 'Oh, what? I wanted to lie in. I'm tired.'

'What you been doing?' asked Karima.

'Nothing,' replied Rico.

'Well. Get up. Let's talk about doing something. I'm coming over.'

Rico reluctantly dragged himself out of bed, to the bathroom, to the kitchen and to the living room, where he waited for Karima. It wasn't long before she turned up. She rang the bell and knocked on the door at the same time. Rico jumped up and ran to the door.

'What's your problem?' he said.

'Thought you might still be in bed. How you going?'

'I was OK until someone got me out of bed.'

'Be cool,' said Karima. 'It's all good.'

'What's good?' asked Rico.

'It's all good,' said Karima. She saw that Rico wasn't in the best of moods, so she tried another approach.

'Hey, so you not pleased to see me?'

'Yes. I just wanted to rest today,' replied Rico.

'You got anything to eat?'

'Of course I haven't got anything to eat. I told you, I just got out of bed.' He paused, smiled, and said, 'We got cake. Sit down.'

They both sat down and they began to drink fruit juice and eat cake. Karima ate as if she was starving, but she didn't let it stop her from speaking.

'So, what did you get?'

'What do you mean?' asked Rico.

'What did you get at court?'

'I didn't get anything. I didn't do anything, they didn't see anything, so they let me go from the station.'

'You're lucky.'

'No, I'm not lucky,' said Rico. 'I didn't do anything – you mean I was unlucky for being arrested in the first place.'

Karima wiped her mouth with the back of her hand and leaned back into the seat.

'Were you still in the police station when it got firebombed?' she asked.

'I was out by then, but I saw it,' replied Rico. 'Do you know who did it?'

'No,' said Karima. 'But whoever did it did a rubbish job. I hate the cops, I hate the whole system. They mess up our lives and when we react they lock us up.'

'Well, you did go robbing shops,' said Rico, reminding her of the fact that she had chosen to go 'shopping'.

'That's not robbing,' said Karima. 'We were just reclaiming stuff. They got me and my crew locked away in a Young Offenders' Unit, they messed with you – so here's what we gonna do. Revenge. We got a plan. We got an amazing network of people on our phones, they're angry, brov, so we're gonna do August all over again. This time it's gonna kick off here in Birmingham. We got north, south, east and west Birmingham covered, so when the city's burning then the rest of the country will kick off. Yes, brov, the last riot is going to look like a street party. This time we're gonna do real extreme shopping, you get me?'

'I get you,' Rico replied. 'But you ain't got me.

What you doing that for? That ain't going to do anything. You'll end up where you just came from.'

Karima became even more animated.

'Look what they done to us, we can't let them get away with it. If we hit them back we can inspire others, and all over the country people will rise up, rob the rich and start burning up cops. It just takes someone to start it and then others will follow. Let's do this.'

'I'm not doing this,' said Rico. 'Trust me, it don't make sense.'

'So what you going to do? Nothing?'

Rico stayed silent, so Karima continued.

'You can't do nothing. These people have been provoking us, watching us and searching us for so long. Wake up, brov. Even you said you're sick of being stopped all the time. The riots sent a message to them, but we got to keep the momentum up, we got to let them know what time it is.'

'It's time for me to go back to bed,' said Rico quite seriously.

'Is that all you have to say?'

'That's all I have to say. No – there's something else I have to say. Don't do it. Smashing a few shops and getting some new clothes is nothing, it's not going to change the world, and, anyway, you can do better than that.'

Rico was not interested in Karima's plan. He never would have been interested in it. Rico hated violence and Karima knew this. The only reason Karima thought he might be interested was because she thought he would be as angry as she was. He was, but he believed in changing the world by non-violent means.

'Are you scared?' asked Karima.

'Of course not. I'm not scared of anything. It's just a waste of time. You go on the streets, cause a few fires, break a few windows, nick a few jeans, and you think you're bad. If you really wanna be bad you'd do something that really makes a difference, not just something that gets you locked up again.'

The expression on Karima's face went from intense concentration to a bright smile.

'You really missed me, didn't you? And you really care about me, don't you?

'Well . . .'

Before Rico could continue Karima threw her arms open.

'Come on. Give me a hug.'

Rico stepped over and put his arms around her. As they hugged, Karima spoke in his ear.

'Sometimes you make me think, you know. But, you know, I got my style, you got yours.'

'That's one way of looking at it,' replied Rico.

'Do you remember the last time I was here?' asked Karima.

'Yes.'

'You got me when I wasn't on form. I'm ready for you now.'

Rico pulled away and went to a corner of the room where he connected a computer game console to the television. They played computer games for two hours. This time Karima was victorious. When the games were over she left, but before she did she checked up on Rico.

'Are you good?'

'I'm good,' he replied.

'No, I mean, you're not going to say anything, are you?

'What you saying, you can't trust me? No,' Rico said defensively. 'I'm not going to say anything, but I still think you should just stay cool and be careful. They're going to be watching you. You got a police record now, and I don't want to see you back inside. That's all I'm saying.'

Chapter 9

Like Father, Like Son?

Thunder roared and echoed and lightning lit up the night, but neither the activities in the sky, nor the rain that was falling heavily outside disturbed Rico as he worked late into the night. He was now running all four of his computers, and he was getting close to completing the website job.

Aware of what his mother had said about not seeing him much, he decided to take a break and join his parents in the living room. It was Sunday night, his parents would normally be watching television together, but when he entered the room the television was on and Stefan was reading a newspaper on his own.

'Where's Mum?' asked Rico.

'She's gone to bed. She's so tired lately. Every time she stopped moving today she fell asleep. She works too hard.'

'I know,' said Rico, sitting down and picking up the TV remote control. 'Is there anything good on?'

'I don't know. I haven't been watching it.'

Rico started flicking through the channels. He liked watching TV documentaries, but tonight there weren't any, none that weren't repeats that he'd already seen. Sunday night television was safe family viewing, films, game shows and talent contests. After he surfed through all the fifty-two Freeview channels he decided to watch BBC world news. He focused on the television, concentrating and trying to understand as much as he could of the issues of the day. It was more of the same. People demonstrating in New York against the shooting of an unarmed young man by vigilantes, women demonstrating for equality in Saudi Arabia, and the aboriginal people of Australia demanding better job opportunities. What really caught Rico's attention was a report that was closer to home. The government was considering passing a new law that meant that all the public's digital communications would be stored and made available to the government or the security agencies. Rico stopped listening to the programme and got lost in thought. He was instinctively against anyone storing his information; for him the Internet represented a space where information and ideas flowed freely, and things were only saved or shared when the creator of the content had chosen to do so.

'I'm just reading about that,' said Stefan. The government wants to know everything about you. It's not good enough for them just to have a copy of your birth certificate, now they actually want a bit of your blood.'

'It's your DNA, Dad.'

'I know. It's the same thing. They got *your* DNA already.'

'I know,' said Rico. 'The first time I got arrested they took it. They said they would destroy it but how do I know they will?'

'They're always watching you, always listening to you, and always taking your money. There's no freedom.'

Rico turned the television off and sank even deeper into thought. Stefan folded his newspaper and placed it on his lap.

'You know what we need,' said Stefan. 'A workers' revolution. The working class should rise up, the unions should unite, and we should just take over. We need mass strikes all over the country – the ruling class can't rule without us, so we should put down our tools and take to the streets.'

'That's so old,' said Rico. 'The workers hardly have tools any more. It should be like, put down your laptops, or put down your smartphones. And as for taking to the streets, look, I go on demonstrations all the time – they're important, but I know they hardly get noticed by those in power. They just stop the traffic for a while and then people go back to their jobs and get on with their lives. The new way should be cyber.'

Stefan pointed to Rico. 'Well, you know more about that cyber stuff than me. All I know is that something has to change, and if you look at history, change has only happened when people have taken to the streets. You were on the streets just last week.'

'Yes,' said Rico. 'There were thousands of us, but I'm beginning to wonder what it changes. I'm fed up of pounding the streets, and speeches about the workers, the people and the unions. We've got to find another way.'

'I agree,' said Stefan. 'I'm just not sure if you're going to find it up there on your keyboard.'

They both stayed quiet for a while, as if they were contemplating each other's point of view. Then out of the blue, Stefan said, 'Just over a week and it's back to school then. Are you looking forward to it?'

'Yes.'

'Really?'

'Yes. What's so strange about that?'

'Nothing. I just thought you might want a longer holiday.'

'I've got work to do, but I'm actually missing school a bit. There's loads of friends I haven't seen for a while.'

'Talking about your friends,' Stefan said, 'how's your friend Karima now?'

'She's OK,' said Rico.

'Good. I like her.'

'Why do you like her so much?' asked Rico.

'She's an individual, she's different, and you suit each other,' said Stefan, smiling.

Rico sat up swiftly. 'Are you kidding? We're good friends, but not like that.'

'I know,' replied Stefan. 'I just really like her.'

* * *

Rico and his dad talked a lot that night. It was the first time they had talked so long for months. By the time Rico got to his room he was thinking about government DNA storage, how to change the world, the purpose of school, and the state of his mother's health. He had so much on his mind that he just went to bed and slept on it all.

Chapter 10

Job Done. Now What?

After Rico had finished the website, he celebrated by going to Telford's, where he worked, and buying himself the biggest external hard drive on the market and some other computer accessories. When he arrived in the shop Ana was on her phone talking to a friend about her birthday plans. It was all about going to a club on Broad Street and dancing into the early hours of the morning. As she spoke Rico smiled, and she smiled back, thinking that Rico was impressed by her party plans – but Rico was smiling because he was thinking of how her birthday was going to be better for reasons other than partying.

After Rico had bought his goods, Mr Telford called him into his office.

'A few more jobs have come in for you. Can you take a look at them before you go and tell me if you can fix them when you're in on Saturday?'

'No problem,' replied Rico enthusiastically. 'If I can't do them all on Saturday and they're not too big I can take some home and do them there.'

Mr Telford smiled. 'I tell you what, lad; you're busier than me. If you carry on like this you'll be buying me out. This place will mainly be a computer repair shop, and I'll just sell a few bits and pieces in the corner.'

'I don't think so.'

'I thought you said you've always wanted to have your own computer business?'

'I do.'

'Well, you've already got the business; all you need is premises, and if I retire there might be a chance of you taking over here.'

Rico almost jumped with delight. 'Are you serious?'

'Of course I am,' said Mr Telford. 'But that's a long way off yet. I've still got some life left in me, and you've still got to finish school. Now go and take a look at those jobs on your workbench.'

Rico checked the jobs that had been left for him – they were all small ones that could be done on Saturday. He said goodbye to Mr Telford and Ana and began to walk towards the bus stop, but just thirty seconds into his walk he was joined by Speech.

'Can you stop a minute?' asked Speech.

Rico looked at Speech and straight away he noticed that there was something wrong.

'What's up?' asked Rico.

'I've got a bit of a problem. How's the website?

'It's done,' said Rico.

'Great. You haven't said anything to her, have you?'

'Hey, man. I told you I wouldn't. Do you wanna see it?'

'Yes,' said Speech, but he didn't sound as enthusiastic as Rico had expected.

'OK then, put this web address in your phone.'

Speech shouted, 'I told you, I don't have a phone!'

'OK,' said Rico. 'Give me a pen and paper.'

Speech handed Rico a small notebook with a

pencil attached to it. Rico wrote down the address and handed it back.

'If you log onto that web address and use that password you can see the site. Only you can see it now, it hasn't gone live yet.'

'Thanks,' said Speech, with his head bowed.

'What's the matter?' asked Rico, who was now beginning to get really concerned.

'I was driving here, and I think I got flashed by a speed camera.'

Rico laughed. 'A speed camera. It's not that bad. It's not the end of the world.'

'You don't understand,' said Speech, with his head still low. 'I've already got nine points. You get three points for speeding, but if I get another three I'll get banned, and I really can't afford to get banned. My family rely on me. I need to drive.'

'Just wait and see.'

'I can't wait and see,' said Speech. 'I can't bear the waiting.'

'But there's nothing else you can do.'

Speech thought for a moment. Then he raised his head and looked at Rico. 'There's something we can do, man. You can help me.'

'How can I help you?' asked Rico.

Speech looked seriously at Rico. 'The speed cameras are run by the Fixed Penalty Office. I don't know if the camera caught me for sure, so I want you to just hack into their systems and see if I'm on their list.'

'No way,' said Rico. 'I'm sure that's illegal or something.'

'Look. This is really important to me. I've got sick relatives up north that I have to look after, I'm the only one in my family in Birmingham who drives, and I've got young kids to look after. I'm not asking you do anything like mess about with stuff. Just go and see if my car registration is on their lists of fines pending. Just let me know and I'll think about what to do next.' Speech took a roll of money from his pocket. 'Here's £300. That's how badly I need this, and I know you can do it.'

Rico looked at the money, then he looked at Speech. 'I'll try, but if I get in I'm not going to do anything. I'm just going to have a look.'

'That's cool,' said Speech, taking out his notebook again. He wrote down the car registration number, ripped out the page and handed it to Rico. 'That's the car reg. Just take a look for me. And here's your money.'

'No,' said Rico. 'I'm not doing this for your money. I guess I'm doing it for your family.'

'Good man,' said Speech. 'I've got to go. I'll find you in a couple of days.'

'How?'

'I'll just find you,' Speech said, walking away.

That night Rico checked the website he had made for Ana and he could see by an internal counter that he had installed that Speech had visited the site. When he knew that his parents had settled down to watch TV, Rico went onto the Fixed Penalty Office website and started to look for weaknesses in their security. It didn't take him long to get into the main servers, and then to generate passwords to get him deeper into restricted areas and to view pending speeding fines. He looked manually for Speech's car registration number but he could not find it. Then he searched for it using his own software, but he still could not find it. Convinced that the car had not been flashed, Rico left the site, covered his tracks, and went to sleep.

Chapter 11

A Change of Mind

'Rico. Rico.'

Rico turned over in his bed.

'Rico. Rico.'

Rico turned over again. He knew that his parents had left for work, so this had to be a voice in his head. Or a character in his dream.

'Rico. Rico. Wake up, brov – I'll ring the bell if you don't.'

Rico sat up in his bed.

'Rico. Come to the window.'

It was only then that Rico realised that the voice was coming from the street outside, and that it was Karima. He got up. Wrapping himself in his duvet he went over and opened the window and shouted down as quietly as he could.

'What's up with you? It's so early. What time is it, anyway?'

'Almost nine,' Karima shouted.

'What you doing here so early?'

'Hey, brov,' Karima said, trying to sound reasonable. 'You think it's early cause you've been snoring for a few hours, and I think it's late because I've been having fun all night. Anyway. I got a problem. Games console. Been on it all night, then it just crashed.'

'So what do you want me to do?'

'Fix it, brov. Do that rebooting, rejigging, reprogramming thing you do and make it all right for your sister.'

'I don't believe this,' Rico sighed. 'I'm coming down.'

Rico opened the front door still wrapped in the duvet. Trying to hold it all together with one hand, he reached out with the other.

'Give it to me. I'll have a look at it later.'

'Can't you check it now?'

'No way. Don't you get it? I'm sleeping.'

'Are you pleased to see me?'

'Yes, but go away. I'm tired.'

'Can I come in then?'

'No.'

'Have you got any cake?'

'No, I've got no cake, and I just said, I'm tired, now go away.'

'No problem,' Karima said, as if conceding. 'Do you think you can fix it for this afternoon?' She grinned.

'I'll try,' said Rico. 'If it's a straightforward crash it shouldn't be a problem.'

'I'll call you later then,' said Karima as she turned and began to walk away, but Rico called her back.

'Hey!'

'What's up?'

'So what's happening with you and your burning-up-the-city plan?'

Karima laughed.

'So, what's happening?' Rico insisted.

'Nothing, brov. I listened to you, didn't I. Like you said, they got me marked already, and I don't wanna spend more time inside. I wanna be free, out here, with you. It's like a life-change thing, you get me? So never mind the negativity, let's play games and eat cake.'

Rico smiled. He was relieved that Karima had changed her mind, and impressed with her attitude, but frustrated that he couldn't tell her about his latest creative adventures, and about how much money he was making. He felt that he had to keep his side of the bargain with Speech and tell nobody, not even his closest friend. Rico could trust Karima with his money, his property, or to be there when he needed her, but he could not trust her with information. She just got too excited and talked too much.

'It's all good then,' said Rico.

'Yeah. It's all good. See you later,' Karima said before strutting off down the street as if she owned it.

Rico crept back into bed but as soon as he woke up he got to work on Karima's game console. He felt personal pride knowing that he had made her change her mind about trying to start another round of riots. He was sure that if she did she would simply have ended up spending a lot more time locked up. Working on the console was a welcome break from the more serious work he had been doing, but it didn't last for long. It was an easy job, a simple case of reinstalling the programme. That evening, Karima came back to pick up her games console. It was now working perfectly.

Chapter 12

The Real Deal

Rico did some small jobs for neighbours over the next couple of days, but he tried to take it easy and prepare mentally to go back to school. He went to work in the shop that Saturday, then after work, as he was walking to the bus stop, Speech appeared in the very same place he had done before. This time he looked like he was back to his normal self.

'I had a look at Ana's website. You've done a great job on it,' said Speech. 'She's going to love it.'

'When's her birthday?' Rico asked.

'In six days. We're almost there. So well done and thanks.'

'No problem. I got her a great domain name and I've come up with a few tricks to make the site easy to find on search engines. Another thing. I checked your car and it's not on there. I checked all the cars flashed by cameras in the last six months, and your car's not there. So you have nothing to worry about.'

'Thanks, man,' said Speech, relieved. 'That's really taken a load off me. You're a good kid. Look, I really need to talk to you.'

'You're talking to me now,' said Rico.

Speech took a step closer to Rico. 'No. This is real talk.'

'What is it with you?' Rico said, stepping away. 'You just appear out of nowhere and you always want to talk to me. What do you want now?'

'Do you remember the subway where we spoke the first time we met?'

'Yes,' replied Rico.

'Let's meet there in twenty minutes,' said Speech.

'What's wrong with just talking here?'

'Trust me. We can't talk about what I want to talk about here. This is big. Very big.'

'I don't know about big. It better be good,' said Rico. 'I'll see you there in twenty minutes.'

Speech walked off in one direction, Rico walked off in another. The subway wasn't far. At normal walking speed he would have reached it in ten minutes, so he took his time, and he still arrived before Speech. He waited, and Speech turned up ten minutes late. Speech's mood had changed again. This time he was serious. No smiles, no greetings, he just started talking.

'You're good at what you do. You care about stuff. You got locked up during the riots, didn't you?'

'Yes, but not for long. They had nothing on me.'

'That doesn't stop them. They got you on their books, they got your DNA, they got you, man,' said Speech.

'I know all that stuff. Big Brother and all that. It's happening, I know, but there's nothing we can do. If they're watching us, we just have to make sure we're watching them.'

Speech nodded his head in agreement. 'You're damn smart, man. That's why I like you. You know what's going on. You got awareness, and you've raised your consciousness. A lot of kids your age haven't. You're intelligent, but you're a bit soft.'

'What are you trying to say?'

'Are you a revolutionary?' Speech asked.

'What kind of question is that?' Rico replied.

'It's a simple question. Are you a revolutionary? Do you want to change stuff?'

'You can call me what you want but, yeah, I want to change stuff.'

Speech kept his eyes on Rico.

'So tell me, what do you want to change?'

'There's so much,' Rico replied. 'Where do I start? Our school is falling down. I'd do something about that. How do they expect us to have a good education if the buildings are falling apart? Every other week my mum has to do more work for less pay – I'd do something about that. I keep getting stopped by the police, and I want to do something about that. I turn on the TV and all I see is war. I know we can't stop all wars but we can stop selling guns all over the world. I'd change the way old people are treated. I'd change the way we treat homeless people, refugees . . . you know, poor people. And most of all I would make sure young people have a say. There's so much.'

Speech interrupted. 'But this is all talk, isn't it? You say all this stuff, but if it came down to really doing something about it you'd run a mile, because you don't know what you're really talking about, do you?'

'That's not true, man. I care about stuff but no one else does. Especially not kids of my age.' Rico was getting angry now.

Speech looked deep into Rico's eyes. 'I might not be your age, but I care,' he said. 'And the truth is, I know you do too – that's why I'm talking to you now. Because you're talented.'

'Get to the point,' said Rico.

Speech continued. 'The cops have been doing what they want to do and getting away with it for years. It doesn't matter which government is in power, it's all the same. That's because all politicians are the same. The best government is no government; the best system is no system.'

'Come on, man,' Rico said, showing his frustration. 'I said, get to the point. I thought you wanted me to do something for you?'

'I do,' said Speech. 'Do you know Lloyd House?'

Rico thought for a while. It sounded vaguely familiar but he couldn't recall it. 'No.'

'It's on Colmore Circus. Not far from here.'

'Of course,' said Rico. 'The police headquarters.'

'That's right, man. The headquarters of the West Midlands Police Force. The second largest force in the country. That's where they live. That's where they plot and scheme. That's where they launch their operations. How about you hack into their computers?'

Rico stiffened and shouted, 'Are you joking?'

'Keep your voice down,' said Speech.

'You want me to hack into the police network?' Rico said, trying to control his disbelief.

'Ah, are you saying you can't do it?' There was a hint of excitement in Speech's voice. His eyes had lit up. 'Think about it, man, it's the ultimate protest. Almost anyone can hack into a supermarket, or an estate agent, but this goes right to the people who administer power over us. This goes right to the people who keep stopping and searching you as you go about your lawful business. You can do this. I know that they have a backup system – they'll spend about ten minutes trying to fix the old system, and if that doesn't work they turn on the backup. So it will be down for ten minutes at the most. But it's not about the time; the point is, they'll lose power for a while. And for the time that they lose control, we are victorious. It's easy.'

'This is madness,' said Rico. 'I don't even know you, and look at the things I've done for you already.'

'Yes, and I'm grateful. But this is not for me.'

'Who's it for then?'

'This is for all of us,' Speech said, waving his hand to the horizon. 'This will be part of a day of protest that many people have been planning for months.'

'How come I haven't heard about it?'

'Because it's an underground thing. It's not being advertised. This is not a student demo. This is going to be a national day of action by really radical organisations.'

'So what else is going to happen?' asked Rico.

'We got people hacking into banks, politicians' websites, loan sharks, even an arms dealer's website. It's all righteous stuff.'

'So what do you want me to do?' said Rico, still uncertain.

'You just have to put their systems down for ten minutes, man. You don't have to change anything; you don't have to take anything. You're just putting them out of action for ten minutes. I know you can do it.'

'Of course I can do it,' said Rico. 'But do I want to do it?'

'Just ten minutes. Come on, man. That's all it takes,' Speech said, trying to reassure Rico.

Rico looked around. He stepped away, rubbing his chin and thinking hard. He thought about all the times he had been stopped by the police for no reason. Then he turned to Speech. 'OK. I'll take it down for ten minutes, but that's all I'm doing.'

'Great,' said Speech, smiling and nodding his head. 'I got information and codes for their website and their internal site – they run on separate systems. Just think of it, cops running around like headless chickens for ten minutes. It will be cool.'

'How long have I got?' Rico asked.

'We need to do it on Monday.'

'Monday!' shouted Rico.

'Keep it down,' said Speech. 'Yes, Monday.'

'But I start school on Monday. Now it's Saturday. That gives me one day.'

'How long will it take you to check it out and see what's possible?'

'I suppose I could do that tonight,' said Rico.

'Well, you do that, and then meet me here at this time tomorrow. If all goes well we should be ready for Monday.'

Speech reached into his jacket pocket and handed Rico a memory stick.

'All the information you'll need is on that. I've

done as much as I can but I need you to just crack the last stage. You'll see what I mean once you have a look, but make sure you keep that stick with you at all times, and make sure you give it back to me. And one last thing. Don't say a word to anyone, not even your closest friend. She's a great girl but we need to keep it tight.'

'How do you know about her?'

'I'm an organiser, Rico,' said Speech. 'I have to know about everything. Just be really careful around her. She can't control her tongue.'

'Don't worry, man. If you know so much, you'll know that I can control mine,' said Rico.

Speech reached out and put his hand on Rico's shoulder. Rico felt uncomfortable but didn't flinch or move away. Speech squeezed and said, 'Great. I'll see you tomorrow.'

Chapter 13

A Protest Like No Other

Rico went home and got to work straight away. His hacking technique was quick, and his work method well tested. It was now just a matter of breaking a few codes, breaching firewalls and working around security systems, and that didn't take long. Rico got in, and got out quickly. Then he got to work on some ideas that would make the hack more creative.

The next day at the appointed time Rico went back to the subway to meet Speech, who turned up ten minutes late again. Again he began to speak without saying hello.

'So what you got for me?'

'I'm all ready. I went onto the network and checked it out. They got good up-to-date security, but I can deal with that. We sell that stuff in our shop.'

'So at a given time it will just go down, will it?' asked Speech.

'No,' said Rico. 'I thought I'd jazz it up a bit. There'll be this big peace sign that will come up on the public website for about ten seconds, and then the site goes down. As soon as it goes down, the internal network gets hit. First a page comes up with a big sunflower for five seconds, and then big words appear saying, "You're under arrest". And then that network goes down.'

Speech rocked with excitement.

'Oh man, you're having a laugh. That's so cool. I like that, I really like that.'

Rico continued. 'They should both be down for ten minutes, then *ping*, up pops a laughing policeman for five seconds, and everything's back to normal.'

Speech's excitement rose even more.

'A laughing policeman? Are you for real?'

Rico broke a sly smile. 'I thought we should have some fun.'

'Too right,' said Speech. 'Fun. Militant fun. Yeah man, that's what we need. Have you got my memory stick?'

'Right here,' said Rico, dipping into his pocket and handing the stick over.

'This is going to be good,' said Speech. 'We're making history.'

'It might be good,' replied Rico. 'But I'm not so sure about making history. Sites are being hacked all the time.'

'Trust me,' said Speech seriously. 'It is good, and you are making history.'

Although Speech was a little strange, and Rico wasn't as excited as Speech, Rico was beginning to feel that the idea of doing a peaceful, humorous cyber protest was a great one, and he was now very pleased that Speech had approached him. His previous hackings had been minor ones – solemn, lone experiences – but now he was part of something bigger.

'We're ready to go tomorrow,' said Speech.

'I just don't get it. I haven't heard about any cyber protest, and I usually know about these things,' said Rico.

'I told you,' said Speech. 'This is real underground

stuff, and you're a part of it. This isn't organised by a trade union, you know, there are no posters on the streets. This doesn't happen until it happens. And it happens at one o'clock.'

Rico stepped back and flung open his arms. 'What kind of time is that? I'll be in school then, and it's our first day back.'

'You don't have to be. Just slip out during your lunch break. You can do that, can't you?'

'I suppose so,' said Rico. 'But I could also stay in school and just programme it so that it comes on at one without me.'

Speech thought for a couple of seconds and then spoke. 'No. I think you should be there, just to make sure. And the timing has to be exact. One on the dot. You can do that for me, can't you, man?'

'I can do that for you, man,' said Rico. 'It's just weird timing. What kind of protest happens in the middle of the day, when everyone's at work – or school?'

'Like I said,' replied Speech, 'this is a protest like no other. It will be cool.'

'But I need to get back to school quickly,' said Rico.

'That's OK. Your lunchtime starts at twelve-thirty, it takes you about fifteen minutes to get home. You got time to relax, take it easy, and do your thing at one, then you got fifteen minutes to get back. Just don't stop and talk to anyone and you will make it in plenty of time. There will be a lot going on. Who knows, you may even get the afternoon off school.'

'What? Are you hacking the school or something?'

'Let's just say – all you need to do is concentrate on what you're doing.'

'OK. Here's what I'll do. I'll hack in, that will take a couple of seconds, and then I'll leave. Their website and Intranet will go down for ten minutes, but I'll just go back to school. The hack closes itself down anyway.'

'That's what we need to hear. How much money do I owe you?'

Rico was quick to reply. 'This is not about money. This is about us. I don't want any money. Just send some work my way when you can.'

'Cool,' said Speech. 'So we're on for tomorrow then?'

'We're on.'

'Good luck, my man,' said Speech, and then he was gone.

Chapter 14

Best Laid Plans?

The first day of the new term started awkwardly. Mr Donavan, the head teacher, spent fifteen minutes addressing the school and talking about the evil people who went on the rampage over the holidays trying to bring society down. Without naming names he mentioned that he had heard that some of them were from this school, but he assured everybody assembled that there would be no riotous behaviour in this school. Then it was off to class and soon it was as if the holidays had never happened, and it was lunchtime.

As planned, Rico left school as soon as the lunch break began. When he got home his mother had just left to start her shift at work. There was still hot water in the kettle. He had reached home with enough time to make a sandwich and a cup of tea, and then he went upstairs. He had left everything on standby so had very little to do. He waited until it was one minute to one, then he typed in some code, and at one second to one he clicked on the mouse and watched it happen.

Peace sign.

Site down.

Sunflower.

Message: YOU'RE UNDER ARREST.

Intranet network down.

He smiled. He wanted to stay to see the laughing policeman, but he had to go. Then the doorbell rang. Rico began to panic.

'Speech,' Rico said aloud. 'It better not be him.'

He thought that maybe Speech had done the ultimate surprise appearance act, appearing at his home. He thought of looking out of the window, but he ran downstairs instead; he was heading that way anyway. He opened the door, convinced it would be Speech, but it was Karima. Rico sighed in relief, and then surprise.

'What are you doing here?' he asked.

'What are *you* doing here?' she said. 'Why did you leave school? I was worried about you, brov. Thought something was wrong.'

'Nothing's wrong,' said Rico. 'I just had something to do. But it's good to know that you cared. Let's go.'

They rushed off back to school and as they parted to go to their classes they made a plan to meet that evening with some other friends and hang out on the streets. Rico thought that by then people would have heard about the various sites going down, or maybe the school site would have gone down too.

The school site didn't go down. Everything was quite normal, until the last lesson of the day. Rico was sitting at the back of the English class when Mr Donavan came in and spoke to Mrs Dovric, the English teacher. Mr Donavan used his hand to shield any words from straying in the direction of the pupils, but from the teachers' expressions it was easy to see that whatever they were talking about was serious. Mr Donavan then turned to the class, looked around and called Michelle Holland out. She was a quiet, blonde girl who nobody knew much about. She stood up and walked to the front of the room.

'Now, class,' said Mrs Dovric. 'I need to leave

you alone for a few minutes. Read the passage we were just looking at and find as many punctuation mistakes as you can. I'll be back in a moment.'

All three left the room and for a moment there was silence, but then the class started to chatter. Most were wondering what Michelle Holland could have done that was wrong. She was such a good girl. Some started to make jokes saying that maybe she was a bad girl after all; they began to make fun of her. Rico just watched and listened.

Mrs Dovric returned, looking upset, but went straight back to her teaching as if nothing had happened. But one pupil shouted, 'Is she in trouble, Miss? What has she done?'

'Never you mind,' Mrs Dovric replied. 'Michelle has had some very bad news, so remember, be nice to her. Now let's get back to work. We do English here, not gossip.'

By home time, word began to spread around the school. As he walked towards the gate Rico overheard one girl saying to another, 'Did you hear about Michelle Holland? A bomb went off at the big police station in town and her dad was in there. He died. It's a shame, isn't it?'

Rico was shocked by what he had heard. He marched quickly to the girl and began to ask questions.

'What happened?'

'A bomb went off at that police headquarters place at lunchtime. Lots of people got killed. Michelle Holland's dad got killed.'

Rico's head started to heat up. 'Are you sure?' He nervously bit on his bottom lip.

The girl spoke hurriedly. 'Everyone's talking about it. It's on the Internet and everything. Her mum came and took her out of school. I saw them both crying their eyes out, getting into a police car.'

'Thanks,' said Rico, walking away and going to a corner of the playground where he could be alone. He was trying to process what he had heard. A bomb, the hack: could there be a connection? He heard a familiar voice calling.

'Rico. What you doing?'

Karima was running towards him. As soon as she got to him she put her arm around his shoulder and continued to speak. 'You waiting for someone?'

'No,' replied Rico.

'So, be seeing you later then?'

'Yes. What we going to do?' Rico asked, trying to sound interested.

'Don't know. Maybe we can go into town.'

'Have you heard about the bomb in town?' asked Rico.

'Yes. But that will be all cleared up by tonight,' Karima said dismissively, but she could see that Rico was thinking deeply.

'Hey. It wasn't me,' Karima said, laughing. 'I told you I ain't on that any more. I'll come round and get you later.'

Karima walked off, leaving Rico on his own. Rico turned on his phone and began to walk home.

Rico's house was not far from the city centre and the police headquarters. He could hear the emergency vehicles as they tried to make their way through the traffic. When Rico arrived on Cavendish Road the first thing he saw was police cars, a long line of them. As he got closer he noticed they were near his house. He turned and walked the other way. As he did so his phone rang. It was his mother.

'Rico. Where are you?'

'What's the matter, Mum?'

'Rico, what have you done?'

'Nothing.'

'The police are here. They're taking all your computers. Come home.'

Rico began to run in the opposite direction from his home. 'I haven't done anything, Mum.'

'I believe you. So come home then, son. The police are . . .'

Another voice came on the phone. It was a man's voice, but it wasn't his dad's.

'Rico. Just give yourself up and we can sort this all out. We just need to talk to you.'

Rico ended the call. It rang again. Rico looked at the caller ID; this time it was Karima. He answered but she spoke so quickly he struggled to keep up with her.

'Brov. The cops are after you. Some people are saying you blew up the cop shop. I said, no, not my Rico. They're saying you did some computer stuff and bombed up the place like you are some big terrorist or something. As if. Where are you, brov?'

Rico ended the call without speaking. He took a while to breathe, and then he turned his phone off. A bus drew up at a stop nearby. He didn't know where it was going, but he ran and got on it.

Chapter 15

The Deliberate Accident?

The bus arrived at a bus station and the few passengers who were left began to get off, but Rico waited until he was the last. He had no idea where he was until he saw a sign above the ticket office. West Bromwich Bus Station. It was busy, mainly with local schoolchildren making their way home. Rico was hungry. He didn't understand what was happening – he was wanted, he was desperate, but the people around him were carrying on as normal. He had very little money. He thought of buying something to eat, but that would leave him with even less money, and unless he gave himself up he was going to need a bus fare. Then Rico had an idea.

There was a trip he had wanted to make for a long time. Maybe this was the time to make it. He tried to avoid eye contact with anyone as he walked around the bus station. He found a map, identified the bus he needed and got on it. When he got off the bus he had to make his way from memory. He was too scared to ask anyone for directions but after a few wrong turns he found the road he was looking for. He hesitated in front of the house. It was such a long shot, but he realised he would soon look suspicious if he continued to just stand outside looking at the house. So he walked up and rang the bell. A woman in her early twenties answered. Rico recognised her, and to his relief, she recognised him straight away.

'Rico. What a surprise. What are you doing here?'

'Hi Kim. I need to find Lola,' he said.

'Why don't you just call her?' she said. 'Haven't you got her number, or is she still not on speaking terms with the family?'

'I've got no problem with her, but I don't have her number, and I just need to find her fast.'

Kim was a friend of Rico's sister, Lola. She invited Rico in, but Rico wanted to know that he wasn't wasting his time.

'Do you know where she is, or not?'

'Of course I do,' said Kim. 'Come in.'

'I can't stay long,' said Rico.

'You can stay for as short or as long as you like,' she said, guiding Rico into the living room. Rico walked in and to his surprise, there was his sister Lola, sitting on the floor eating a pizza out of a box. She jumped up and hugged him.

'Rico! What's up, little brother?'

'What are you doing here?' Rico couldn't believe his eyes.

'I live here now. Decided to move in with my friend, didn't I? She needed some company, and we were spending most of our time together anyway. But the real question is, what are you doing here?'

Rico looked at Kim, unsure if he should say anything, so he just said, 'I've got problems.'

'And I've got to go out,' said Kim, sensing that Rico might appreciate some time to talk to his sister alone.

When Kim left the house Lola offered Rico a piece of her pizza, then watched as he ate the rest of it at speed. Rico told Lola everything, and when she asked questions he answered them as honestly as he could. Until Rico's arrival she had not heard of the bombing. She told Rico that she and Kim had a television set but very rarely used it. She turned it on, and almost every station was covering the incident. They both sat down and watched in horror as they viewed the scene of the bombing. News reporters from all over the world were standing in front of cameras. In the background the destroyed police headquarters could be seen, with the whole of the reception area blown out. Firefighters had just put out what remained of the fire, rubble was spread all over the road, and staff that had been trapped in the building were being led out. Many of them were injured.

Lola's jaw dropped, she shook her head, and tears ran down Rico's face.

The police had no doubts. They told the media that they were looking for Rico Federico, the young mastermind behind the bomb plot. He was reported as being a computer fanatic and very anti-police. It was also said that he had links to an Islamic group and could have been working on their behalf. The police were desperate to find Rico and so they released a narrative of what they believed had happened.

"From the activities recorded in his computer we can see that Rico Federico had been spying on the police, and so he knew the exact time, each week, when sterile equipment would be delivered by courier to the headquarters for use by scenes of crime officers. For security reasons this equipment is X-rayed and scanned in by bar code, but when the equipment arrived this afternoon it could not be processed because our computers were down. We can see from his computer records that it was Rico Federico who compromised our computer systems. After placing the delivery on the counter, the courier told the officer that he had to go back to his vehicle to call his office and notify them of a possible delay. We now know that this courier was an imposter, the real courier having been delayed by a deliberate accident. The imposter went back to his vehicle, but drove off, and exactly one minute later the bomb went off. Neither the imposter nor the vehicle can be traced. This was a well-planned, professionally executed operation. Rico Federico is a dangerous person. We believe he is still in the Birmingham area. The public are warned not to approach him if they see him, but to report any sighting of him to the police."

Rico put his hands together in front of his chest as if praying. 'I didn't know anything about a bomb,' said Rico. 'Lola, you have to believe me. Honest, I just thought it was a game. You know, hack in, close down their site, and have a bit of a laugh. I didn't know anything about a bomb.'

Lola saw that his tears were real. She could see his hands shaking as he pleaded to her. She put her arm around him. 'I believe you.'

'What shall I do?' Rico asked, looking at the carpet.

'First of all, take some time to think. Why don't you call this Speech guy and see what he has to say?'

'He's gone,' said Rico. 'And I haven't even got a phone number for him. He said he didn't have a phone.'

'Any idea where he lives?'

'No.'

'Email?'

'No,' said Rico. 'I haven't got anything for him.

He just used to meet me in the streets. It was like he just knew where I was all the time.'

Kim came home, hurried through the door, and went upstairs, shouting down as she ascended.

'Lola. Can I have a word?'

Lola ran upstairs.

'Lola,' Kim said anxiously. 'I got something to tell you. It's about your brother.'

'I know,' said Lola. 'It's complicated.'

'Complicated?' Kim was shouting now. 'Complicated? Nine people are dead, twenty in hospital. And your brother did it!'

'He didn't,' said Lola. 'I know him. He wouldn't do something like that. He is my brother. Come downstairs. He'll talk to you. He's got nothing to hide.'

Lola persuaded Kim to calm down and go and listen to Rico. Downstairs, Rico retold the whole story again. It was tedious, but he wanted to make sure he got every detail right. Kim was convinced by Rico but she was also convinced that he should give himself up straight away.

'It's the most honest thing to do,' said Kim.

'But who's going to believe me?' said Rico. 'I've been set up. I'll be on my own.'

Lola looked at Kim, then she looked at Rico.

'You are not alone. You have us. Kim will be here tomorrow, and I'm going to take the day off, so let's all get some sleep and we'll decide what to do tomorrow.'

'Good idea,' said Kim. 'My head's hurting.'

Chapter 16

Blood is Thicker Than Water

Rico slept on the couch but got very little sleep that night and in the morning he had stiff shoulders, a stiff neck and a headache. Kim and Lola weren't feeling much better either. They had slept in their beds, but they had also spent many hours talking about the situation they had found themselves in. As they sat eating breakfast from plates on their laps they compared the strength of their headaches then, for the first time, Lola asked how her parents were.

'They were OK the last time I saw them,' said Rico. Then he thought about how panicked his mother sounded the last time he heard her, and of how confused his father would be. His head flopped down and he continued to speak with his head bowed. 'But I'm sure they're not OK now. Not after what I've done to them.'

'Hey. Let's talk about something else. Have they been bad-mouthing me?' Lola asked, half-smiling.

'No. They haven't really been talking about you at all.'

'Good.'

'Why is that good?' asked Rico.

'Because I'd rather have them not talking about me than have them bad-mouthing me. I've had enough of them bad-mouthing me. Just because I wouldn't do what they wanted me to do.'

'I thought you fell out with them because they didn't turn up to your graduation,' said Rico.

'Yes. No,' replied Lola. 'Well, kind of. There's more to it than that. I wanted to study Art at university, but they convinced me to do Law. I wasn't crazy about the idea but I thought, OK, that might be useful, you know, get a law degree, then go out into the world and help people. I really struggled to stay on top of my studies and had very little support from them and, yes, they didn't turn up to my graduation when I really wanted them to. But what really got me was, the day after I graduated they showed me a photo of some guy from Spain that they wanted me to marry.'

'What, Mum and Dad did that? Who was the guy?' asked Rico.

'I don't know. I'd never seen him before, and I never wanted to see him again, and never wanted to hear such rubbish again. Actually, it was more Dad than Mum, but when I told them I wasn't interested in this guy they said they had another one lined up. As if I'd done all that study just to be married off. So I've never forgiven them for not thinking about what *I* want from my life, and they've never forgiven me for calling them old-fashioned and backward.'

'I didn't know any of that,' said Rico. 'I thought they were modern and up-to-date and everything.'

'Yes, but you're a boy. Don't get me wrong. I don't think they're bad people, I just think they treated me badly, and I guess I wanted to punish them for it. I don't hate them; if I really hated them I wouldn't make contact when I do.'

'That's not very often, is it?' said Rico.

'Well, I'm busy working in the art gallery and

making a life for myself. I just like them to know sometimes that I'm still alive.'

Kim interrupted. 'Hey, enough of going down memory lane. We have a lot to think about. Rico, I've thought about this all night and I still don't know what you should do. You could stay here for a while, but you are wanted: they are not going to stop until they find you, so I think I have to ask again: why don't you just give yourself up?'

Rico stood up abruptly. He walked around in a small circle in the middle of the room. 'Because. Because – if I give myself up now I'm on my own, and who's going to believe me? I know you both said I'm not on my own and you'll support me and all that, but when they have me in the station I'll be all on my own, so I'm going to wait for a bit.'

'Wait for what?' asked Kim.

'I'm going to wait for a while to see if they get Speech. I'm sure they will, and once they get him the truth will be out.'

'But,' said Lola, 'it doesn't matter if they find him or not, you'll still be in trouble.'

'Yes, I know,' said Rico loudly. 'But I won't be in as much trouble. There's a big difference between doing a bit of computer hacking and mass murder.'

Lola responded quietly. 'I might not have actually practised law, but I think they might be able to get you on conspiracy to mass murder. I don't know, I'm just saying.'

Rico sat back down. 'How can they do me for conspiracy when I didn't know what was going on?'

'It gets all technical; they can twist things using jargon. All I'm saying is that something that makes sense to you might not make sense to the law, or vice versa.'

'Vice versa, vice versa!' Rico said angrily. 'Who cares about vice versa; I'm telling the truth. That should be good enough.'

'I'm just telling you what it's like,' said Lola, now raising her voice. 'So don't get angry with me.'

'Calm down, both of you,' said Kim. 'Let's be constructive.'

The room went silent as they all began thinking. Soon the silence was broken by Rico.

'I know. I can hack into the police computers again and send them a message, or I could just send them an email telling them everything that happened.'

'That's mad,' said Lola.

'What's the point of that?' asked Kim.

'Well, they would know the real story,' replied Rico. 'And once they knew the real story, they'd let me go.'

'You know that's not going to work,' said Lola. 'As soon as you contacted them they would find out where you were and then they'd raid us.'

'OK, you're right,' said Rico. Then he had another idea. 'Lola. Why don't you go home and see what's happening? See how Mum and Dad are, and see if they know I'm innocent.'

'Rico, you're not exactly innocent,' replied Lola.

'I am.'

'You're not. You hacked into police systems. It doesn't matter how you did it and why you did it, it's illegal. You even told me before I left home that you'd hacked into other stuff, and I did warn you. But you didn't listen to me.'

'I did listen to you,' said Rico. 'I know it's illegal, but I thought it was a bit of fun. I've been hacking for ages and never hurt anyone. I just wanted to see things. I just wanted to test my skills. I wouldn't have hacked into the police if I knew what was really happening. I know that doesn't make it right.'

'It doesn't make it right,' said Lola. 'And it's no excuse. The point is, you're not innocent.'

'So what are we going to do?' asked Kim impatiently.

'What about my idea of you going home, Lola?' asked Rico.

'No. That's not happening,' replied Lola. 'Anyway, it would look strange if I suddenly turned up.'

'Phone them then,' Rico said sharply.

'No,' said Lola. 'What are we going to talk about? I'd have to tell a pack of lies about not seeing you, and if the police are watching then they'd trace the phone call and . . .'

'But,' Rico interrupted, 'it probably looks strange that I'm all over the TV and you haven't made contact to ask what's going on.'

'They'll just think I don't care.'

'You don't, do you?' shouted Rico.

Lola lost her temper and really shouted.

'If I didn't care I wouldn't have taken the day off to be with you. If I didn't care I wouldn't have been up all night worrying about you. If I didn't care . . .'

'OK,' said Kim. 'Let's all calm down.'

The sound of a cheap computerised version of Mozart's *Allegro* filled the room. It was Lola's phone. She answered.

'Oh, I'm sorry, I forgot – we both forgot – can we go next week?'

She put her hand over the phone and whispered over to Kim, 'It's Hutch – it's about tonight.'

She continued the call.

'There's stuff I need to do so I just can't make it tonight. No, it's not really convenient for you to come over here – we're really busy. Look, let's talk in a couple of days – I'll call you – maybe we can see each other this weekend. OK, great, thanks, bye.'

'Who was that?' asked Rico.

'It was Hutch, my boyfriend; we were going out tonight. I forgot all about it.'

'So did I,' said Kim. 'What did he say?'

'He sounded a bit let down but he's OK. I think he's blaming himself.'

Rico turned to Kim. 'So do you have a boyfriend?'

'I did but I soon got rid of him,' Kim replied.

Lola continued, 'He was an absolute horror. She kicked him out, then I moved in.'

'Never mind my life,' interrupted Kim. 'Let's

deal with this. I think these ideas are stupid, Rico. You have to give yourself up.'

'I need more time,' said Rico.

'He needs more time,' Lola said to Kim. 'And you need some clothes,' she said to Rico.

'He needs some what?' asked Kim. 'What's clothes got to do with it?'

'Well, look at him,' replied Lola. 'Those are basically his school clothes. Too recognisable. Whatever happens, he's going to need a change of clothes.' She turned to Rico. 'I'll get you some clothes. You can pay me back later.'

'I still think we need to deal with the whole situation, not just the clothes,' said Kim, looking unhappy.

'Of course we need to deal with the whole thing,' said Lola. 'But we don't want to rush and make the wrong decision. So I suggest we leave Rico here, go for a drive into town, and get him some clothes.'

'OK,' said Kim, turning to Rico. 'What's your size?'

Lola and Kim went shopping. The house fell silent and Rico was left alone with his thoughts.

Lola drove to a budget clothing store and they bought the first things they saw that didn't look like school uniform. When they had finished shopping for clothes they went to a chemist and bought a toothbrush and a comb. They drove home, but halfway there the mood changed when Kim raised her concerns.

'We have to be careful, Lola. The more we do to help him, the more we get ourselves involved in this, and this is so serious. We could be getting ourselves into real trouble. We could be part of a terrorist plot.'

'This *is* serious,' said Lola. 'But my little brother is no terrorist. He's just got himself into a situation and he needs our help.'

'You mean he needs *your* help.'

'What are you saying?' asked Lola. 'You don't want to help him?'

Not wanting to upset Lola, Kim thought carefully before she spoke. 'I'm saying he got himself into this mess, so he can get himself out of it. He might have to go to prison. You know that, don't you? And if he does, I don't want him to take me with him. That's all I'm saying.'

'Imagine you were in this situation. You'd want someone to help you.'

'But I wouldn't get myself in this situation.'

'Come on, Kim. He's fifteen. We all make mistakes.'

'Yes,' said Kim. 'But if we make mistakes, we should put them right. He should give himself up.'

'That's up to him, but whatever he does I have to stick by him,' said Lola.

'But I don't,' said Kim, looking straight ahead and unable to look at Lola.

'And what does that mean?' Lola shouted.

'Lola, I'm sorry. You are my friend, but Rico is not my brother, he's yours. It just means I have to think of the bigger picture. That's all I'm saying.'

The rest of the journey home was tense, with Kim staring out of the window as Lola drove, neither saying a word. When they arrived home Rico could sense that something was not right, but Lola put on a smile.

'Hey, try these on. They looked great on the hangers.'

They handed him the bags and went upstairs to their rooms, leaving him to get changed. Kim began to play loud music on her computer. It was unusually loud, and after a few minutes, as Lola was going to the bathroom, she heard talking coming from Kim's room. It was Kim's voice, but she was speaking quickly and quietly, trying not to be heard over the music. Lola put her ear to the door to hear what Kim was saying.

'I can't turn the music down,' said Kim. 'They might hear me. He's here now, downstairs. The terrorist kid. Rico Federico. He stayed here last night. I know hoax calling is illegal, I know that, but I'm telling you the truth. Come quickly and you will find him here now.'

Lola ran to her room. She opened a drawer where she kept her underwear and pushed her hand right to the back, grabbing a handful of banknotes that she had hidden there. She then went to another drawer where she kept earphones, batteries and other bits of gadgets, and she grabbed an old mobile phone connected to its charger. She stopped at Kim's bedroom and heard Kim still on the phone, now giving out their address. Lola ran downstairs. Rico stood up, pretty pleased with the clothes he was now wearing.

'Not bad,' he said. But he saw the panic on Lola's face, and heard it in her voice.

'You've go to go, Rico,' she said. 'Look, here's some money, and here's a phone. Don't phone home with it, and don't phone me with it. I'll call you. But you got to go. The police are on their way.'

'How do you know?

'There's no time for that now. Just go. I'll call you. Grab what you need and go.'

Rico put his new baseball cap on, and on top of that he put up the hood of his new hoodie, then he stuffed some of his old clothes into one of the bags, with the money, phone, charger, toothbrush and comb, and he went. Just as he was going through the door Lola pulled him back. She hugged him tightly. 'Take care.'

'I'll try my best. Thanks, Lola,' said Rico. 'I'll sort it out.'

Lola ran upstairs and went straight into Kim's room. Kim was still on the phone.

'How could you?' Lola shouted. 'How could you? You couldn't even give us a bit more time to sort things out.'

Kim shouted back. 'This is my house, and I'm responsible for what goes on in here. I'm scared, Lola. I don't want any of this.'

The man on the phone could be heard calling out. 'Hello? Hello? Are you still there? Hello?'

'You're evil!' shouted Lola.

'At least I don't kill people,' said Kim.

Chapter 17

Road Block

The road was closed off. People were ordered to stay in their houses, and no one was allowed to enter the street. Armed police surrounded the house. Some officers were in the back garden, others were in the front, and some were in the neighbouring gardens. There was no escape route. The occupants of the house were ordered by loudhailer to come out, with their hands above their heads. The door opened slowly, the armed officers set their sights on it, and the two frightened young women came out. They held their arms up high. Lola looked straight ahead; Kim was crying, but she was able to speak.

'Please don't shoot us.'

A voice spoke using a loudhailer. 'Is there anyone else in the house?'

'No,' said Kim. Lola just shook her head.

'Walk forwards,' said the voice.

They reached the pavement and were told to stop, then a group of armed police officers stormed the house. Lola's car was searched and inside the house the police went from room to room looking in every corner, in every cupboard. As each room was checked an officer would shout 'clear'. When they found no one in the house they all left. An officer shouted, 'All clear.'

Lola and Kim were told to stand still as a female officer approached them. After searching them she asked whose house it was.

'Mine,' said Kim.

'And who called the police?

'I did,' said Kim.

The officer went and spoke to the officer in charge of the operation and the armed police were told to down their weapons. Lola and Kim were taken inside and the road was reopened. Two male uniformed police officers stood outside the house, and one male and one female plain-clothes officer went inside to question Lola and Kim.

Lola and Kim sat together on the couch as they were being questioned. The male officer sat in front of them, the female officer stood next to him. Kim and Lola were both honest, but they only answered the questions they were asked. They told the officers how Rico had turned up unexpectedly the night before, how they fed him, where he slept, and that he told them he didn't do the bombing. When asked why they didn't tell the police as soon as he arrived they explained that at first they didn't even know about the bombing, but when they found out, many of their conversations were about when he should give himself up.

The policeman warned them that if Rico were ever to show up again they should tell the police, and just before they left, the policewoman asked one final question.

'It's in your best interest to be completely honest. We understand that you didn't know what was going on and you weren't sure what to do. We also appreciate that it was you who called us, but this is now a terrorism and murder case, with national and possibly international implications, so we need to know. Do you know where he is?'

Lola and Kim had disagreed over how to handle Rico's arrival, they had even shown their disagreements in front of the police officers, but they were both telling the truth when they said they didn't know where Rico was.

Chapter 18

A Friend in Need?

Rico had £185.55. He had clean clothes on, dirty clothes in a bag, one mobile phone that he couldn't use, and a mobile phone with a charger that he could. After leaving Kim's house he just walked as far as he could; he had no idea where he was, he just wanted to get as far away from the house as possible. He found trying to move around in streets that he didn't know, whilst trying not to be noticed by anyone, very difficult. Fortunately there were lots of teenage boys around who looked like him, but he still didn't want to draw attention to himself. Speaking to someone wasn't going to be easy; in this part of the West Midlands they would notice his accent. The Birmingham accent wasn't very different, but it was different enough to be noticed. It was getting late though, he was hungry, and he had to eat. As he wandered through some back streets he saw a fish and chip shop. He didn't like fish and chips, but he was in no position to be choosy. He didn't want to go into the shop himself for fear of being recognised, so when he saw a young boy texting on his phone he approached him.

'You all right, mate?'

'Yeah. You from round here?' asked the boy.

'Yeah, I'm from just over the road,' Rico said, pointing. 'But I got a bit of a problem.'

'What?' said the boy suspiciously.

'I got banned for fighting in the fish shop last week; they won't let me back in there. Could you get me a bag of fish and chips and a drink? I'll buy you a bag of chips.'

'Who were you fighting?'

'A boy from Stourbridge. He thought he was hard, pushing me around, so I let him have it.'

'Good. I don't like boys from Stourbridge. Who won?' asked the boy.

'I did. Think I broke his nose. Anyway, they

banned me. Can you do it for me?' Rico said, not wanting to make the conversation drag on.

'You'll give me a bag of chips?'

'Yes.'

'No,' said the boy. 'I'll do it for a bag of fish and chips.'

'OK,' said Rico, not wanting to argue.

'No,' said the boy. 'I'll do it for a bag of fish and chips and a drink. Just like you're having.'

'That's a lot,' said Rico.

'That's my final offer,' said the boy.

'OK,' said Rico. 'You can have a bag of fish and chips, and a drink. Just like I'm having.'

He gave him £10 and the boy was soon back, carrying two bags of fish and chips, two cans of drink, and the change. He handed Rico his food and drink and his money.

'Any time you need chips I'll get them for you. Where you going now?'

'I'm going home. See you, maybe.'

Rico began to walk away.

'Hey,' shouted the boy. 'You're going the wrong way.'

Rico realised he was walking in the opposite direction from where he had said he lived. So he quickly thought of a reply.

'I'm just walking round the block to eat my food before I go in.'

'I'll come with you.'

'No,' said Rico as he quickened his pace. 'I like to eat alone.'

It didn't take him long to finish his meal, and then he was left with a major challenge. He had to find somewhere to sleep. He considered bus stations and cheap hostels, but he thought they would be too risky. Eventually he found a housing estate. He thought about sleeping behind a large group of rubbish bins, but it was a mess, and he could see by the unfinished meals there that he would probably have to share the space with hungry rats from the neighbourhood, feral cats or even a fox. He walked to the back of the estate. It was a dead end. He jumped up, grabbed the top of the wall and pulled himself up, just enough to see over, and although it was dark he could make out that it was an allotment. He lowered himself back down, rested for a couple of seconds and then jumped up again, this time pulling himself right up until he was on top of the wall, and then lowered himself down on the other side. He was at the back of the allotment and hardly needed to go anywhere before he came upon a row of sheds. The first few he tried were locked, but then he found one that was open. He searched around in the dark. Running his hands along the wall he came across rakes, hedge trimmers, spades and forks, and a watering can. Then he found a large woven bag used for garden waste, and he knew exactly what he was going to do with it. He made a bit of room for himself in the corner of the shed and sat down. With his back upright against the shed wall he took the bag and covered his legs.

It was a long night. As Rico lay awake he started to imagine all types of spiders crawling over him. Although he could feel the tiny spider feet walking across his forehead, down his neck and in his ears, it was his mind playing tricks. When he was tired of thinking, tired of worrying and tired of the mind games, his head would drop, he would sleep for a short time, and then he would suddenly snap awake again. He did this time and time again until dawn, and he got very little sleep.

The shed was still dark but Rico could see light trying to enter through cracks in the wooden panels and the space under the door. He opened the door just enough for him to see out, and to let enough light in. He had a good look around at where he had slept, and then at the tools and equipment, but none of it was of any use to him. He looked outside and saw a couple of early risers tending to their vegetables. They were in the distance, but he knew that whoever owned the shed he was in could come at any time, and he didn't want to be there if they did. He put the bag that he had used to keep warm back where he found it, along with the other things that he had moved. He brushed himself off, hooded himself up, and was ready to go, although he had no idea where. Before he left he stood behind the door and turned on the mobile phone that Lola had given him. He waited awhile, but there were no messages. He stared at the phone trying to will a message to arrive, but none came. As he looked at the phone display saying NO MESSAGES, he felt desperately lonely. There was no one to turn to. He turned the phone off. He waited until the people in the allotments were looking the other way, and left. He retraced his footsteps and climbed back over the wall into the housing estate.

* * *

The housing estate was just coming to life with people leaving for work and school. Rico walked through the estate and back onto the streets, but he was nervous. He knew that the longer he was on the run the more people would know about him, and the more people knew about him the more difficult it would be to hide. As he walked he made mental notes of the road names and his direction of travel, whilst at the same time trying to hold his head down. Then he saw a sign for Dartmouth Park; he followed it, and then more signs, until he reached the park. He wandered around the park for a while until he saw a lake. At various points around the lake people were preparing to do some fishing so Rico sat and watched them. He watched for an hour as more people came to feed the ducks and swans, and although none of them paid any attention to Rico he began to feel uneasy. He stood up and began to wander around again, and then he saw some toilets. He quickened his pace and went straight to them. After relieving himself he went to the sink where he brushed his teeth, and when his teeth were done he dropped his hood, took off his cap, and washed his hair using the hand soap. After he had washed and rinsed he put his head under the hand dryer to let the warm air dry his hair. He was feeling relieved, relaxed and refreshed – until he was disturbed.

'I could think of easier ways of cooking your head if that's what you really want.'

Rico twisted round and looked up to see a man standing over him. He was dressed in overalls and carrying some gardening tools.

'I fell over,' said Rico. 'Got some dirt in my hair so I washed it out.'

'As long as you didn't mess up one of my flower beds that's all right,' said the man with a grin.

'No,' said Rico. 'It happened by the lake.'

'Good job you didn't fall in then. You would have needed a bigger hair dryer than that.'

The man continued into the lavatory. Rico's hair was now dry but he kept his head under the dryer until the man had left the lavatory altogether. As soon as he left Rico took his bag and went back into one of the cubicles. Rico was relieved that the man had not recognised him, but he began to wonder how long it could continue. When would his luck run out?

Rico sat on the closed toilet seat, wondering what he should do next. He turned on the phone to see if there were any messages. There were none, so he quickly turned the phone off. In his mind he began to relive the moment he closed the police website down, and then the moment he saw the police outside his house. Then he recalled watching the news report on TV with Lola, when he realised just how much damage had been done. He shook his head, trying to shake the pictures out of his mind. He was desperate to hear from Lola, and he couldn't understand why she had not been in contact yet. Then he thought that maybe it was time to stop thinking about Lola; maybe she had given up on him. Maybe he should just start thinking about himself, and his own survival, alone.

It was almost midday. Rico had seen enough of the toilet cubicle, and he was getting hungry. He waited until the lavatory was empty and left. His plan was to find a way of getting something to eat, even if it meant more fish and chips, but as he made his way out of the park he felt a thud in his lower back. It hit him so hard he dropped his bag. He thought of running but when he looked behind him all he saw on the ground was a football. He looked up and saw a young man running towards him. He looked beyond the man and saw another younger man waiting for the return of the ball so they could continue their kick around.

'Sorry, mate,' said the man. 'Are you OK?'

'Yes,' said Rico quickly. 'I'm OK.'

'Really sorry, mate. We didn't mean it, honestly.'

'It's no problem,' said Rico nervously, kicking the ball back.

The man picked up the ball, but after he picked it up he carried on running towards Rico, stopping right in front of him. The man was panting and out of breath.

'I got a powerful kick, yeah, but I'm just not very good at getting it on target.'

'It's cool,' insisted Rico. Having not wanted to draw attention to himself, this was exactly what was happening. People were looking his way, concerned about Rico after seeing how hard he had been hit.

'It didn't even hurt me,' said Rico, stepping around the man and waving goodbye to him.

'OK. See you,' said the man, who then turned and ran back to his mate.

Rico continued walking out of the park but just before he got to the gate the ball appeared again. This time it rolled past him. He looked behind him and saw the same man with his companion running towards him. Rico picked up the ball and kicked it back to them. The man caught the ball but they both continued running towards him. By the time they got to Rico they were both out of breath. The man with the ball was visibly excited, his friend less so.

'What's your name?' asked the man.

'Why do you want to know?' replied Rico. He continued to walk. Rico was now very anxious. He just did not want a conversation with these people. He forced a smile. 'Don't worry. I told you, I'm fine. I've been hit by footballs much harder than that.'

'Come on. Just tell me your name,' the man said a little more forcefully. 'Be polite. My name's Rohan, what's yours?'

Rico went silent. He wasn't sure what to do. Then Rohan looked to his companion, threw him the ball and said, 'I told you. It's him. The terror kid. I know his face.'

Rico began to run. He ran out of the gates and down the street. The men ran after him. Rico was not a fast runner, and having to hold the bag slowed him down, but he ran as fast as he could. Then suddenly a man spread his arms open and blocked

Rico's path. Rico tried to run around him, but the man was big, and there was nowhere to go.

'I've got him!' shouted the man. 'No one gets past me. I used to play rugby. No one got past me then, no one gets past me now.'

The man wrapped his arms around Rico until the men caught up.

'Did he steal something from you?' asked the man. Rico tried to struggle free, but the man gripped him so firmly he could barely breathe.

'No,' said Rohan's companion. 'We're just playing a game.'

'Just playing a game?' said the man disbelievingly. 'You could have fooled me.'

'It's OK,' said Rohan. 'Let him go. He's our friend.'

'Your friend. I'm sorry,' said the man as he let Rico go. 'And there I was, trying to be a superhero. You young ones play some strange games nowadays. I'll be off then. Leave you to your strange games.'

The man walked off. There was an audible sigh of relief from all three of them. The men looked at Rico, and Rico looked at them, none of them sure what to do next.

'So it's like this, right. I'm Rohan, and this is my brother Dean.' Rohan lowered his voice. 'We know who you are, but don't worry, there's no problem. We're cool. We not gonna tell the cops or anything. Let's go for a walk. Get off the busy road.'

The two brothers stepped either side of Rico and began to walk. Rico had no choice but to walk with them.

'What are you going to do to me? asked Rico, who was now a little scared.

'Nothing,' said Dean. 'We are your friends. We're on your side.'

Rohan and Dean were older than Rico, in their twenties. Rohan had blond hair and was skinny, tall and very talkative. His brother Dean was also blond, but a man of few words. Both wore jeans and West Bromwich Albion football shirts. When they had left the main road Rohan continued to talk.

'I can't believe you're here. Hey, do you need anything?'

'Are you going to call the police?' asked Rico quietly.

'No way!' said Rohan. 'We hate the police. Do you need anything?'

'I just need somewhere to rest and something to eat.'

'That's no problem,' said Rohan. 'We can help you with that. Can't we, Dean?'

'Yes,' said Dean. 'Shall we take him to the pub?'

'That's what I'm thinking,' said Rohan with a big smile on his face.

'I'm not going to a pub,' said Rico.

'It's not that kind of a pub. Well, it's not a pub. You'll see when we get there.' said Dean.

They walked for a short while until they came to Dean and Rohan's house. Dean went in, leaving Rohan and Rico to walk on and wait a short distance away. Soon Dean appeared from the side gate, signalling them to enter. Once through the gate Dean and Rohan led Rico to a cabin at the bottom of the garden. It was comfortable inside, with three armchairs, football shields and trophies on the walls, a pool table at its centre, and a bar that looked exactly like a bar in a pub.

'You can stay here for a while. No one comes here, not without our permission anyway,' said Rohan.

Rico looked around at the trophies, and then he walked up to the pool table and ran his fingers over the cloth.

'I see why you call it the pub now.'

Rohan joined him and started to run his fingers over the table.

'Yes, when we were small we liked to play pool.'

'And drink,' said Dean.

'So our dad made this cabin for us,' Rohan continued. 'It's a great place to just chill out. We don't normally let people in here, you know. But you're special.'

'What do you like to eat?' asked Dean

Rico reply was quick. 'Right now, I'll eat anything.'

Rohan drew the curtains and Dean went back into the house and brought back some sandwiches, biscuits and two cans of soft drink. The brothers watched as Rico cleaned up the food that was placed before him, then they talked. They talked for most of the afternoon, and come early evening the brothers went into the house for their meals, leaving Rico for a while, returning again with more food.

When they talked it was about life in the area, what the local kids were like, films they had seen and football, which Rico was not at all interested in. The brothers explained that their mother was disabled, and although she could walk a little around the house, most of the time she had to use a wheelchair, and their father didn't go to work but spent most of his time looking after her. Rohan was doing most of the talking, but what was making Rico uncomfortable was the fact that they didn't mention that he was on the run. Not until late in the evening when they were getting ready to leave him for the night.

'We have to turn the light off now; if we leave it on it will look weird. Don't worry, it's safe. No one knows that you're here and no one will find you. Can you manage in the dark?' asked Rohan.

'Of course,' replied Rico. 'I slept in a garden shed last night. Compared to that this is luxury. Can I charge my phone up?'

'No problem, just do it in the dark. Don't open the curtains until we come back, and try to be quiet. But you'll be fine.'

As soon as they left, Rico turned on the phone that Lola had given him, but again there were no messages. He was tempted to turn on his own phone but he knew that once he turned it on he could be traced. He put his newly acquired phone on to charge, spent some time thinking, and then he curled up in an armchair and went to sleep.

Chapter 19

A Bit of Cash Here,
A Bit of Cash There

Rico slept soundly right through the night and most of the morning. It was almost eleven o'clock when he woke up. He was hot. The sunlight hit the window and, even with the curtains closed, the greenhouse effect began to fry him. He stood up and as he stretched the cabin door opened, just enough for Rohan and Dean to peep in.

'Can we come in?' asked Rohan.

'Of course,' said Rico.

'We've come over a couple of times but you were fast asleep. We didn't want to wake you up.'

Rohan was carrying a dish, a spoon and a bottle of

milk. Dean was carrying a box of breakfast cereal, a couple of white bread rolls and a jar of jam. Soon Rico was eating the food, with Rohan and Dean looking on. When Rico caught their eyes they smiled back at him as if they were really happy just to see a hungry boy being fed. When Rico was finished they both left, saying they would be back very soon.

Thirty minutes later they returned. This time they were smiling but empty-handed.

'Rico,' said Rohan. 'Our parents have gone down the day centre, let's go in the house.'

Rico was cautious. 'Are you sure?'

'It's safe,' said Dean. 'They're away for a couple of hours. More space in there.'

'You can get all you need,' said Rohan. 'You can go to the toilet, have a shower, anything. Let's go.'

They guided Rico into the house; it was small, but with some surprises: two canaries sang in one birdcage, and there was an owl asleep in another. There was also a big fish tank full of tropical fish and in the corner was a large television.

'Can I watch some telly?' asked Rico.

'Later,' said Rohan.

'I want to see what they're saying about me.'

'Don't worry. We'll come to that in a while.'

Rohan gently put his hands on Rico's shoulders and turned him towards the stairs, then led him straight to the bathroom.

'Do what you like. There are towels, shampoo; we even got nail cutters in the cabinet next to the mirror. It's all yours. Just give us a shout if you need anything else – and take your time.'

Rico spent forty minutes in the bathroom, and when he came out he felt and looked like a different person, but he sensed there was something wrong. Rohan and Dean were being too nice to him. He asked to watch some TV again and the subject was changed quickly. They showed him old family photos in an album, and newer family photos on a laptop computer. Rico feigned interest in order not to upset his hosts.

Back in the cabin they started to talk about the obvious.

'They're looking for you everywhere, you know?' said Rohan.

'I know,' replied Rico.

'You're a bit of a hero, you know?' said Dean.

Rico shook his head.

'No, you got that wrong. I'm no hero.'

'What are you saying?' said Rohan. 'You're the man, you're the one everyone's talking about. Terror Kid, that's what they're calling you, and everyone's scared of you.'

'"Terror Kid,"' Rico said, surprised.

'Yes. The most dangerous kid in the country, public enemy number one. If they get you you're going away for a long time, a very long time, but you're safe here. We have a plan.'

Rico raised his eyebrows and looked at the pair, his eyes darting from one to another.

'What plan?'

Rohan went and stood by the door; Dean went and sat right next to Rico and began to speak.

'We'll help you as much as we can but if you want to survive out here you're going to need some money. We haven't got much but we know where to get some.'

'I've got some money,' said Rico.

'How much?' asked Rohan.

Rico wasn't sure if he should tell them, but he had already said too much.

'About a hundred pounds.'

Rohan laughed.

Dean continued to speak quietly and calmly.

'You can't survive out here on a hundred quid. You need more. We need more, and we're not even on the run. We have a plan to raise our financial status, but we need you.'

'What do you need me for?'

'You know how to make big bombs, and we need a little one, a little tiny baby one.'

Rico jumped out of his seat.

'I don't make bombs!' he shouted. 'That wasn't me. Do you hear me? It wasn't me!'

Dean was unmoved. 'So what you on the run for?'

'It's complicated, I can't explain now.'

'There's no need for you to explain. Sit down, and let *me* explain.'

Rico sat down slowly and Dean continued.

'There's this shop you see, and in this shop there's sweets and cigarettes, and chocolates and magazines, and there's a cash point. This cash point is a bit stubborn. It's not the cash point's fault. The problem is they put it in the wall, and it's concreted in.'

'Why are you telling me this?' asked Rico.

'We've done a dry run so we've got a way into this shop,' continued Dean. 'So we want to go in, and take that cash machine away. But we need you to make a little baby bomb, just enough to blow it off the wall, and trust me, everything will be all right.'

Rico shook his head and spoke firmly. 'I told you, I don't know how to make bombs.'

Then Rohan joined in.

'Hey, man. Whatever you call that thing you made that ripped the cop station apart, that's what we want. That was top class, but we're not in that class. We don't understand politics, we're not freedom fighters or anything like that. We're just poor people who need a bit of money to make life better for us, and at the same time we can help you. You just make the thing, tell us how to use it, and then you wait here. We'll go, do the job, come back, give you a cut, then you do anything you want. If you want to stay here, you can; if you want to move on, you can. You can do whatever you want to do – you'll have the money for it.'

Dean took over.

'It's easy. Come on, look what we've done for you.'

Rico jumped up again. This time he really shouted.

'Yes, you helped me, thanks, but I didn't make a bomb, so forget it.'

Without warning, Dean lost control. He punched Rico on the side of his head. Rico went to the floor. Dean jumped straight on him, put his hands tight around his throat, and shouted at him as he shook Rico's head violently from side to side.

'After all we've done for you! If it weren't for us you'd still be walking the streets. We could turn you in any time, we could grass you up, but we just ask you for a bit of help. You don't help us but you help your Muslim friends.'

Rohan hurried over and pulled Dean off Rico.

'Cool down, Dean. Just chill, man. Go and see if Mum and Dad are back.

Dean got up and left the cabin, cursing as he went.

Rico was stunned by the attack. Rohan helped him to his feet and sat him back down. The inside of Rico's head was spinning, the outside felt as if a brick had been implanted in it. After sitting in a chair next to Rico and giving him a bit of time to recover, Rohan began to try to persuade Rico again.

'Sorry about that. Sometimes Dean just goes crazy, and he's got a bit of a temper on him. Listen, everyone in the country knows how good you are. We just need a bit of help. We're not big-time, we do a little job here, a little job there, make a bit of cash here, a bit of cash there, we're just small-time hustlers. Now, you can help us, can't you?'

'I can't,' said Rico very quietly.

'Well,' said Rohan. 'I always try to be reasonable. I like to talk things through, but Dean's not like that. You've seen how he can just lose his temper. He's desperate, and when he's desperate he's dangerous. I don't know if I can protect you if he loses it again. That's all I'm saying. Come on, do this for us.'

Rico sat looking at the floor. He thought so hard he could feel the electricity in his brain. He was trapped, and he could see only one way out. He nodded his head. 'OK.'

'Good,' said Rohan. 'Now what do you need?'

'First of all I need to rest my head,' said Rico.

'I understand,' said Rohan smoothly. 'I'll go and have a word with Dean. I'll make sure he won't be doing that again, but you will help us, won't you?'

'Yes,' said Rico. 'I'll do it. I just need some petrol and some – some – some fertiliser. I'll do it.'

Rico didn't really know what he was talking about. He thought that petrol ignites, and he had heard on the news that fertiliser can blow up, so he said the first things that came into his head to make Rohan go away. To Rohan it was music to his ears. Rico sounded like he knew what he was talking about. Rohan smiled a smile of satisfaction.

'We can get that stuff. You get your head together and we'll come back and have a chat. How does that sound?'

'OK,' said Rico. 'Yes, we can do business.'

As soon as Rohan left, Rico grabbed a bread roll and gathered his few things together. He opened the curtain just enough to see Rohan enter the house. He thought quickly. Getting out of the entrance at the side of the house was risky; the gate was too near the house. Climbing over the side fence was also risky; he could be seen from the house. So he got his bag, opened the door and slipped round the back of the cabin where he couldn't be seen. Then he jumped over the fence and ran through the garden that backed onto the house behind. He ran to the side entrance gate, but there was a dog. It was small dog, a very small dog, but it was loud and angry. Rico ran with the dog barking at his heels, but when he got to the gate it was locked. Panicking, he threw over the bag, climbed over, picked up the bag and ran along the side of the house, down the street. Once he hit the street he just ran as fast as he could, as far as he could.

Chapter 20

Room Service

When Rico could run no further he stopped to get his strength back. He saw a phone box, picked up the handset and put it to his ear to make it look like he was making a call, and used the time to rest. When he was fully recovered he took out the mobile phone that Lola had given him and turned it on. This time there was a message. He felt weak with relief. It was from Lola, and it was a simple message, and she was using a name that only Rico would know.

It's Woodpecker. Meet me 2nite @ 9
outside the potters house. CU. X

Rico had no idea what the 'potters house' was. He ate the bread roll that he had and spent the next few hours walking from one phone box to another, until he found one with Internet access. He was tempted to check the Internet and chat rooms to see what everyone was talking about, and he thought of checking his emails, but he knew that was dangerous and would leave a trail, so in the end he just put the coins in and searched for 'The Potters House'. It was a church and community centre, and he worked out that it wasn't too far away, so he carefully planned a route and began his journey. Once he had checked the road names and direction of travel he put his head down and went purposefully on his way.

He arrived at The Potters House and waited outside the main entrance. He wasn't sure how Lola would arrive, but within two minutes she pulled up in her Mini. The passenger door opened and he got inside. Lola leaned over, put her arms around his neck and rested her head on his shoulder, whispering in his ear.

'I'm really sorry – Kim just doesn't understand. She's a good friend but sometimes she just thinks about herself.'

'It's OK,' he whispered back.

Lola released him and he put his bag in the footwell of the car and buckled his seatbelt.

Lola spoke as she began to drive.

'After you left, the police surrounded the house and questioned us. It was scary. It wasn't normal police. They came with guns and everything. We didn't say anything though – well, we couldn't, we didn't know where you went – but, Rico, they're serious. I'll help you as much as I can, but you're in big trouble. They're now saying that you might have left the country and gone to an Al Qaeda training camp in Yemen.'

'What, Al Qaeda! This is really out of control. What next? Where are we going?' asked Rico.

'Not far.'

Lola drove down a few side streets, checking her mirrors to make she wasn't being followed, and after a short drive they arrived at a hotel. She parked the car in the car park.

'OK,' said Lola. 'I've already checked in, we have a twin room, you're my brother, and your name is Alex Robinson, and my name is Jill Robinson.'

Rico was nervous. 'Is it safe?'

'It's easy. You don't need to check in. Just go

where I go but look like you know where you're going. It's a big hotel, with a big reception, so no one's going to notice you – unless you draw attention to yourself.'

'OK.'

'Right. Let's do it,' said Lola.

They entered the hotel and Rico stuck with Lola as she walked past the reception to the elevator. Their room on the fifth floor was small, with two single beds, a television and a small table with two chairs squeezed in. Lola's bag was already on her bed. Rico threw his bag on the floor and jumped onto the other bed, lying down and stretching as far as he could. Then, sitting up swiftly, he said, 'I need to watch some TV.'

'Why?'

'Because I want to know what's going on. I'm so out of touch.'

'You're supposed to be. Where have you been sleeping?' Lola asked.

'I was in a horrible shed one night, and in a slightly nicer shed the next night. Turn the telly on.'

'In a while – but tell me more.'

'The first one was someone's garden shed. I don't

know whose. Then last night I slept in a kind of cabin thing at the bottom of some guys' garden.'

'Which guys?'

'Just some guys I met. They recognised me and took me in, but they wanted me to go robbing with them.'

'Rico! As if you're not in trouble already. You didn't say yes, did you?'

'Of course not. Well, I said yes just to give me a chance to get away. Look,' Rico said, pointing to the bruise on the side of his head. 'One of them punched me. They were weird.'

'Are you OK now?'

'Now that I'm away from them, yes.'

'As long as you're OK. Do you want something to eat?'

'Yes, at last, some real food. Where from?'

'Room service. Just make sure you're in the bathroom when they bring the food in. We don't want to risk any staff recognising you.'

Lola ordered a large meal and when it arrived Rico did as he was told and hid in the bathroom. As they ate the meal Rico told Lola everything that had happened over the past couple of days, and how he had felt worried that she had not made contact earlier.

'I had to make sure I wasn't being watched or followed, so I couldn't call straight away. And I couldn't risk calling from my phone with my SIM card, so I had to buy a new SIM card and a cheap old phone. If I call you again it will be from that number. And I'll be Woodpecker, just like in the old days.'

'I understand. So how is Kim?' Rico asked.

Lola's surprise was obvious.

'You sound like you care.'

'I do. I understand her too. She doesn't know me, so she doesn't know if I really did it or not.'

'But she knows me; she should trust me,' said Lola.

'She doesn't know me, and it's her house, so I can understand her not wanting anything to do with me.'

'You're such a considerate guy,' said Lola.

'Apparently I'm a mass killer. Can I put the telly on please?'

'OK,' replied Lola. 'But remember you're a compassionate guy, and not the guy they are making you out to be.'

* * *

Rico turned on the television and began to flick through the channels. The bombing was the number one issue on all the news channels, and the commentators seemed in no doubt that Rico was guilty. Not a participant in a bigger plot, not someone who had been used by people more experienced, but the planner, the organiser and the executioner. When one of the stations began to show interviews with relatives of the dead and injured, a photo of Rico appeared. Of all the photos that could have been used, like school photos or personal photos, the photo they chose to show was one of him looking very tired on an anti-war demonstration. Rico stared at the image, hardly recognising himself and the evil personality they were describing. Lola told Rico to turn the television off. He turned it off and stared at the blank screen but in his mind he could not stop seeing images of the bombing victims and that image of himself.

'What shall I do?' he said.

'I've given it lots of thought and I still don't know. It's up to you. I don't want to sound like Kim but why don't you just consider giving yourself up and just telling them the truth?'

'I've thought about it, but no way. If I give myself up they're going to charge me as if I'm a big murderer. I'll go to prison for the rest of my life. I can't give myself up. I have to wait until they get Speech, then they'll understand, everyone will understand. They need to find Speech.'

Lola pleaded, 'Rico, they're not even looking for Speech, they're not looking for anyone else, they're only looking for you.'

'There must be something I can do.'

'If you give yourself up at least you can try to prove your innocence. If you don't you can't.'

'Lola!' Rico shouted. 'Are you saying that I should give myself up?'

'Well,' replied Lola very gently, 'I'm just saying you should think of all the options.'

Rico thought for a while and Lola watched him thinking. The silence was long. He then turned to look at her. 'I'm not going to give myself up. I can't. Are you still going to help me?'

'I'm your sister, and I'll support you in whatever you want to do.'

'Thanks, that's good, that's really good. Just what I want to hear. But you know what? I don't have any idea what to do.'

Lola leaned forward and began to stack the empty plates on the table.

'If you really want to lie low for a long time, I think I can sort something out, but I need a bit of time. I've booked this room for two nights. I have to go to work tomorrow; the next day, Saturday, is when we have to check out, but I won't let you go back on the streets.'

'Where can I go then?' Rico asked.

'Leave it to me.'

The next morning Lola left for work, putting the DO NOT DISTURB sign on the door as she left. Rico spent most of the day in bed watching television. At first he watched news reports about him, but when he had had enough of himself he went to a film channel for escapism. Lola came back at six o'clock straight from work. She had an Indian takeaway and some fruit with her, and as they ate, Lola began to speak.

'Today's my last day for two weeks. I'm taking my annual leave. I have to rush home now – I have some things to do, and Kim is expecting me – but I'll be back tomorrow morning to check us out and take us away.'

'Take us where?'

'That doesn't matter now, but we're going to get far away from here, up north. I've rented a really remote place for a couple of weeks and we can go there for a while.'

'And then what?' asked Rico.

'I don't know, but let's get away from here first and then think what to do next.'

Rico rushed over to Lola and hugged her. 'Thanks so much. I don't know what I'd do without you. I really don't. Just get me out of here so I can sort out my head.'

Chapter 21

My Name is Rico Federico

Rico spent the evening alone, and although he spent much of the time watching news stations he was more relaxed. In the morning he woke up refreshed. After getting his things together he sat on his bed waiting for Lola. Using the remote control he turned the television on and began to watch the news again. The first thing he saw was a weather forecast, and then the next item rocked him.

"A young girl has been arrested in the case of the police headquarters bombing. Police have taken the unusual step of getting permission from a court to name the juvenile girl in the hope that it will jog people's memories. It is now believed Karima Yussuf used her extremist ideas to inspire Rico Federico. She has been arrested several times previously by the local police, including recently in the Birmingham riots. She was arrested in the early hours of this morning. Witnesses say it took a number of officers to restrain her. Although she was unarmed she violently resisted the arrest."

As the newsreader read the bulletin a picture of Karima appeared on the screen. Rico couldn't stand it. He turned the television off. The hotel phone rang. It was Lola.

'I'm in the reception. I'm just about to check out. The car is right in front of the hotel entrance. Just cover up, come down, walk straight out and get straight to the car. It will be unlocked. I am checking us out. Rico . . . Rico . . . are you there?'

Rico was still thinking about Karima and could barely focus on what Lola was saying. After a short silence Rico replied.

'Yes.'

Lola could sense that something was wrong but all she said was, 'OK. See you in the car.'

* * *

Rico did exactly as he was told, and it wasn't long before Lola appeared. She jumped into the seat next to Rico and turned the car engine on before she spoke. She was pumped up and ready. 'Right. That's all done. Let's go.'

Rico turned to look directly at Lola.

'Take me to the police station.'

Lola turned the engine off and hit the steering wheel with her fists. 'What?'

'Take me to the police station. I want to give myself up.'

'Have you gone crazy or what? You kept telling me you didn't want to go there. I've made all these plans to keep you out. And now you *want* to go there?'

Rico didn't take his eyes off her. 'Sorry, but this is important. I'm not crazy, I've just had enough. I'm really sorry for messing you about. You've done so much to help me. You've always done loads to help me, even when I was a little kid. But now too many people are getting involved. They've arrested my best friend, and she hasn't done anything.'

Lola started up the engine again. 'Are you sure you don't want to wait . . .'

Rico screamed, 'I said take me to the station.

If you don't, I'll just go by myself. I've got to go now! Right now!'

Lola interrupted. 'OK, Rico, calm down. It's cool. I just want to make sure you know what you're doing. Don't worry. If you want to go, I'll take you there.'

She began to drive. 'How do you know about your friend?'

'I saw it on the telly. Her name's Karima. She's like my best friend and she hasn't done anything.'

'Yes,' said Lola. 'I heard something about her on the radio, and something about the shop you worked in being raided.'

Rico shook his head in despair. 'You see? It's too much. The people who are being hurt by this are the people who are least guilty. So let's go, and not just to any station – take me where they know me, close to home. Take me to Summerfield Police Station.'

Lola stopped the car a block away from the station and turned to Rico.

'How do you want to do this?'

'I just want to walk in – alone.'

'Let me come with you.'

'No. Too many people are being dragged in already.

166

If you come in with me they'll probably arrest you too. No, leave me here and I'll go in alone.'

'Are you sure?'

'I really mean this. I've never been more sure about anything in my life.'

Lola leaned over and hugged him. He gave Lola the bag with his clothes and the phone and charger that she had given him. As he got out of the car Lola also got out and went round to the passenger side to hug him again. This was a long, tight hug. They were cheek-to-cheek and Rico could feel tears running down her face, and as she spoke, the movement of her jaw spread the tears onto his face.

'I believe everything you say, and no matter what anyone else says, the truth shall set you free.'

Rico's cap was on, but his hood was down, and still no one recognised him as he walked to the station. He walked straight up to the desk. The Enquiry Officer put down what he was doing and addressed Rico.

'Yes, young man, what can I do for you?'

'My name is Rico Federico. I've come to give myself up.'

The desk sergeant leaned forward and took a

good look. Without taking his eyes off Rico he picked up the phone in front of him.

'I need officers out here to make an arrest.'

He put the phone down and pointed to Rico.

'Now you stay right where you are,' he said.

Rico was nervous but calm. 'I'm not going anywhere.'

A side door opened and two plain-clothes officers came out. They were mid-conversation when they looked at Rico. Without saying a word they both ran towards Rico and took him down to the ground. Rico was struggling to breathe under the weight of the two officers.

'Don't move,' said one officer.

'I can't,' said Rico.

'Good,' said the officer. 'Well, you're under arrest for terrorism and murder. You do not have to say anything, but it may harm your defence if you do not mention when questioned something which you later rely on in court. Anything you say may be given as evidence. In other words you're nicked.'

Chapter 22

More Questions than Answers

Rico sat impassively at the desk as the officer who'd arrested him walked into the room and sat down in front of him. He was called Detective Inspector Kennedy. They were alone in the room, but Rico knew that the small black balls on the ceiling, in the corners, were cameras, and they were probably being watched and filmed by a much bigger group of people. The officer slowly leaned over until Rico got a strong whiff of stale sweat and old aftershave.

'Come on, let's start a conversation here.'

Rico didn't move. 'Come on, let's get me a lawyer here,' he said.

'No problem. We can do that.'

'Well, do it,' said Rico. 'I know I have the right to one, or an appropriate adult. So let's do that.'

'Of course, I'll sort that for you, but it doesn't matter who's here – your people or my people – first of all, me and you have to have a rapport going on. We're going to have to trust each other. After all, we're going to be spending a lot of time talking to each other.'

Rico turned to look at the officer. 'I don't trust you, and you don't trust me; we are not friends, associates or anything, so just give me my rights. I'm a juvenile. I want a lawyer and my parents, and that's it.'

'OK,' said DI Kennedy, straightening up. 'That's the way you want to play it.'

The officer left the room to join his colleagues – eight of them – in an adjoining room.

DI Kennedy had lots of experience in questioning terrorists and hardened criminals, but none in questioning intelligent fifteen-year-olds. He talked to his squad outside the interview room for a while and then agreed that it was time to call Rico's legal representative. DI Kennedy took a pad and pen from his shirt pocket and went back in to see Rico.

'OK. So what's your lawyer's name then?'

Rico was silent. He tried to look confident. He knew his rights, but he didn't know any lawyers.

'Come on, what's your lawyer's name?'

Rico looked up at him. 'I haven't got one.'

The officer laughed. 'So after all the big talk you don't even have a lawyer. Don't worry, we can get one for you.'

'No way,' shouted Rico. 'I'm not having one of your lawyers.' Rico's words echoed around the room. He wanted his parents to get a lawyer for him, but he was also worried about what his parents would think. Would they believe him? Would they stick by him? He needed help, but he wasn't prepared to accept it from the police. 'Give me a phone call,' he said. 'Let me call my parents, and they'll get me a lawyer.'

Rico was allowed a phone call. He called his father and tried to start explaining what had happened, but his father told him not to say a word, and in less than thirty minutes his mother and father arrived at the station. He could hear his father before he could see him.

'If any of you put a hand on him I'm having you.

He's no terrorist and you know it. I'm telling you lot, treat him with respect.'

When they entered the room Lena ran straight to Rico and hugged him. Stefan continued to speak loudly.

'Rico, have any of them touched you? Don't be afraid to say, now. Have any of them laid a hand on you?'

'No,' replied Rico over his mother's shoulder.

'Right,' said Stefan. 'We're going to get you a lawyer and we're going to get you out of here.'

'Have you eaten?' asked Lena.

'Yes, Mum,' replied Rico.

'Are you sure?' asked Stefan.

'Yes, Dad,' said Rico. 'I don't need anything to eat, I just want you to know I didn't blow that place up.'

'We know,' said Lena. 'You don't have to tell us that.'

'That's right,' said Stefan. 'You don't have to tell us that.'

'I've got nothing to hide,' said Rico. 'I'm going to tell them everything I know. I didn't do it.'

'Play it by the book, son,' said Stefan. 'Just do what you have to do and we'll get you out of here.' He turned to DI Kennedy. 'Hey, you,' he said, pointing his finger. 'You can't question him until he has a lawyer. You know that, don't you?'

'Do you have a lawyer?'

'No. Never needed one. But we'll get one.'

'We can help you find one, if you would like us to.'

'No, thanks; we would not like you to. We don't need any help from you. We'll find someone for him.' He turned to Rico. 'Just hang on. We're going home now and we're going to find the best lawyer around. Nothing but the best. That's what you'll get.'

Rico's parents left and he was taken to a cell accompanied by four uniformed officers. Outside the cell they took the laces out of Rico's shoes, and the belt from his trousers. For the first ten minutes he stood in the centre of the cell and looked around. On the ceiling he saw more small black balls containing cameras, and as he scanned the cold, grey concrete walls he wondered how long such walls would surround him. To the left of him there was a toilet, and to the right of him there was a slab that protruded from the wall, with a pillow-shaped hump. It took him a minute to realise it was a bed. He went over to lie down, but when he put his head on the 'pillow' the smell of the toilet opposite the bed overcame him and he stood up immediately. He shook his head and exhaled through his mouth and went back and stood in the middle of the cell. There he stood for over an hour before the cell door opened and he was led away to another room.

This room was a little more comfortable than all the other rooms he had seen. The walls had posters advertising volunteering groups, mental health organisations, dyslexia organisations, domestic violence helplines and drug addiction helplines. He was told to sit down on one of the three leather chairs that were placed around a desk, and he was left alone. Two minutes later a young, smartly dressed black man entered. In one hand he was carrying a small computer case, in the other a grey folder. He walked straight up to Rico and reached over the desk to shake his hand.

'Hello, Rico. My name's Jackson Jones. I've been asked to represent you. Is that OK with you?

He was polite and gently spoken, but Rico was cautious.

'Did the police send you?'

'No. I can assure you that the police have not sent me. I received a phone call from your father, Mr Stefan Federico. Can I sit down?'

'Of course.'

Jackson Jones sat on a chair to the side of Rico. He took his computer out of its case and put it on the table. He opened his folder and took out some papers that he also placed on the table.

'You are now going to be interviewed. I will be here with you all the time, but it's really important that you understand what your rights are. If you feel that you don't want to answer a question, or that you can't answer a question, simply say "no comment." If you don't understand a question, just ask for the question to be repeated. Don't feel intimidated by the jargon; if for any reason you are confused, refer to me. Like I said, I will be here all the time, and I'm here for you. If I feel that a question is unnecessary, unreasonable or unfair, I will intervene. Is that all clear?'

'Yes,' replied Rico. Jackson's confidence helped ease Rico's confusion. The future was still unsure, but at least now he had someone on his side who knew the law.

* * *

Jackson Jones left the room and called in DI Kennedy. The officer entered, sat right in front of Rico and put a CD recording device on the table. He turned it on, and as soon as Jackson Jones sat down the officer started his questioning. For the records he stated his name, the time and date, then addressed Rico.

'We have reason to believe that you, possibly with the help of others, delivered a bomb to Lloyd House police headquarters. The bomb had a timer that was set to go off at a given time, and it did, killing nine people and seriously injuring many others. But we'll come to that in a while. First, can you tell me what your religion is?'

Jackson Jones intervened straight away. 'There doesn't seem to be any reason for you to know my client's religion. Is that question relevant?'

'We believe that the people behind the bombing were religious fanatics, so it would help to know if he has any religious beliefs.'

Jackson Jones turned Rico. 'It's up to you if you want to answer.'

'I'll answer,' said Rico. 'My parents are Orthodox Christian, but I've never been to church.'

'So being an Orthodox Christian doesn't mean anything to you then?' said DI Kennedy.

'Not a thing.'

'Is that why you converted to Islam?'

Rico's eyes shot wide open. He fell back into the chair. 'What? Where have you got that from? I haven't converted to Islam.'

'Your friend Karima Yussuf – she's a Muslim, isn't she?'

'Is she?' replied Rico.

'You know she is. She's a powerful girl, isn't she? She's got a strong will, she's got drive and she's got personality. Did she convert you?'

'I'm not sure if she's a Muslim, and she didn't convert me. Where is she?'

'Do you miss her?'

'None of your business.'

'Was she your girlfriend?'

'No, and that's none of your business either.'

Rico was then questioned about his love of computers, his previous arrests and his attitude towards authority. DI Kennedy's strategy was to try to get Rico to open up about himself, but Rico was always on his guard, and although Jackson Jones looked young, he was confident and not intimidated. Rico was happy that Jackson was there to intervene.

DI Kennedy leaned back on his chair until it was on two legs, stretched, then let the chair drop back onto four legs again and rested his elbows on the table.

'Right. You got arrested during the riots, you were taken in, and you were questioned by Detective Constable Glen Holland. You were released without charge, but you were pretty angry with DC Holland. You knew his daughter Michelle, she was in the same class as you at school; somehow you worked out when he would be at the front desk, probably using your computer wizardry, and you and your friends got together and exacted revenge. Not just on DC Holland, but on the other officers who died that day, and the whole system as you see it. That's how it is, isn't it, Rico? We know what you have done, we know why you have done it – so just own up and let's get this over with. Things will work out easier for you if you make it easier for us.'

Rico was stunned. He felt as if the ground was moving below him. He took a deep breath and looked around the room. He hadn't realised that Michelle Holland's dad was a cop – he didn't really know Michelle Holland – but he could see horribly clearly why the officer was thinking the way he was. DC Holland was the officer who questioned him on the night of the riots. He could see that if they thought Karima was an angry Muslim militant, and he was her boyfriend, then they would think that he had a motive. He hung his head and tried to keep calm so he could gather his thoughts and think clearly. Then he raised his head, looked straight at the officer and spoke.

'OK. I'm going to tell you everything.'

The officer adjusted the recording device so it was closer to Rico, and smiled with satisfaction. Jackson turned to Rico.

'I suggest that we have a moment to speak in private. You don't have to say anything right now.'

'No,' said Rico. 'I know what I'm doing. Yes, I'm guilty. I'm guilty of digital trespass, and hacktivism, and I'm guilty of keeping secrets, but I'm not guilty of terrorism. I don't like cops, and they don't like me, but I'm not guilty of murder or terrorism. So let's talk. I'm ready.'

'You really don't have to speak,' said Jackson urgently.

'I want to speak,' replied Rico. 'I am not a terrorist

and I have nothing to hide. I'm not a bad person, I'm not evil. So let's talk.'

The officer sat back in his chair. Jackson took notes, and Rico told the story once again. He ended by saying, 'I've done some bad things, I've told some lies. I've done all kinds of stuff, but I didn't deliver, plan, or even know about that bomb.'

Chapter 23

Free Speech

After Rico had told DI Kennedy everything he knew, he endured two hours of relentless questioning; Jackson Jones needed to intervene frequently, and the questioning only stopped once for a short break after Rico had asked for a drink of water. Rico answered all the questions as best he could; he was steadfast and not intimidated by the process. He knew that he was telling the truth. Despite everything that Rico said, the officer was still convinced that Rico, fuelled by his anger against the police and inspired by the charisma of Karima, had masterminded the bombing. The officer told Rico that they had checked hours of CCTV footage, all the telephone calls on

Rico's mobile and house phone, and conducted detailed forensic examinations of his computers and belongings, and as far as they were concerned there was absolutely no evidence of the existence of an adult called Speech. It was then that it dawned on Rico that the reason Speech didn't carry a phone was because it would let him be traced. He began to tell the officer his thoughts when the officer interrupted him, banging the table with the side of his fist.

'Look, Rico, we've looked at your computer history and we know that you hacked into your school website. Even before you supposedly ever met this Speech person you hacked into a bank, the local council, the NHS computer systems and Birmingham Airport's website, and you did that all on your own.'

'You're right,' Rico shouted back. 'I did, but that was just me messing around, that was just me being nosy. Can't you see that I've been set up?'

'You haven't been set up. You've done the setting up!' shouted DI Kennedy.

'No, I've been set up!' Rico shouted.

'You set it up, and we're going to prove it,' said the officer even louder.

Jackson threw his pen onto the table. 'That's it.

I suggest we have a break. I need to consult my client.'

'Very well,' said DI Kennedy, standing up and walking out. 'Twenty minutes.'

When the officer had left, Rico burst out.

'I'm sorry if I'm not doing this properly, but I just want to get it all out. I'll tell them all they want to know, because I know if they get Speech this nightmare will all be over.'

'I understand,' said Jackson. 'However, I have to tell you that the protocol is that you simply answer questions that you are asked and don't just offer up information. But I understand this is very emotional for you.'

'That's right. It's emotional, and I just want it to be over with.'

'Are you happy to carry on with the interview?' asked Jackson.

'I wouldn't call it happy, but I want to carry on.'

'OK,' said Jackson. 'As you say, but I won't let them carry on too long.'

'What do you think will happen?' asked Rico nervously.

'It's difficult to tell. They'll probably charge you

with some computer crime so they can hold you and continue investigations.'

Rico thought for a moment. 'Well, that might give them time to find the truth.'

There was a pause. Rico took a good look at Jackson and then asked, 'So are you an expert in this thing then?

'What thing?'

'This terrorism thing.'

'Not really,' replied Jackson. 'When I was at school I saw a lot of injustice, especially with young people. I saw how kids could be abused, exploited and misrepresented. I even saw a teacher get killed, and I wanted to do something about it, so I studied law. I now specialise in defending young people.'

'So how do you know my dad then?' asked Rico.

'I didn't. Not until today,' replied Jackson. 'I'm a friend of your sister, Lola. We studied at the same university. She called your dad, your dad said he needed a lawyer, so he called me, and I came straight away. By the way, Lola asked me to say hello. She said she'll come to see you as soon as she can.'

Rico looked around the room as he tried to put it all together in his head. Then a uniformed officer put her head around the door and said, 'Can you finish up, please?'

'We're just finishing now,' said Jackson.

DI Kennedy entered the room, sat down on his chair and turned on the recorder. Another officer stood at the door.

'Right,' said DI Kennedy. 'The good news is, I'm going to end this interview. The bad news,' he continued, 'is that you are going to be charged.'

Rico's eyes widened in shock and darted from the officer to Jackson, and from Jackson back to the officer.

Jackson spoke. 'I take it that these charges relate to computer crime.'

'I'm afraid not,' said the officer. 'Rico Federico, I am formally charging you with the murder of Detective Constable Glen Holland, and committing an act of terrorism.'

'What?' shouted Rico.

'This is outrageous,' said Jackson.

'I'm afraid this is the way it is,' said DI Kennedy. 'We have consulted the Crown Prosecution Service, and they have agreed with our analysis that there is enough evidence to charge. I have to say at this point that there is a high possibility that further charges will follow.'

Rico could not take his eyes from the officer. He felt like screaming, he felt rage, he felt anger, but all he could do was stare, panicking, as DI Kennedy turned off his recorder and began to leave the room.

As he reached the door he turned back and said, 'You've got ten minutes.'

Rico's eyes stayed on the door after it had closed behind the officer. Jackson gave him time to gather his thoughts. Rico shook his head slowly and turned to Jackson.

'So what happens now?'

'They'll keep you in custody until you appear in court, and I will start preparing your defence.'

'You'd better go then,' said Rico despondently.

Jackson gathered his papers together, put his laptop in its case. He stood up and looked down at Rico, who was now sitting hunched with his head bowed.

'Don't worry,' said Jackson. 'We're going to do the best we can for you.'

'When will I see you again?' asked Rico.

'I will come back tomorrow and we can talk

about the individual charges and how you choose to plead. Then on Monday morning you'll be in court. It will be a very short court hearing, but I'm going to try to get bail for you. It will be difficult, but I'll try.'

He reached forward and shook Rico's hand.

'Thanks. Thanks a lot,' said Rico.

Jackson picked up his papers and laptop and left. Rico gazed at the walls surrounding him. He was alone with his many thoughts racing around his mind.

Chapter 24

Friends Disunited

Rico was not alone for long; soon DI Kennedy entered the room with another officer. An officer Rico had not seen before. They were both smiling in a way that made Rico feel uneasy.

'Right, let's take you away.'

Rico stood up and they took him by his arms and led him towards the cells – but they walked past the cells and came to the door of another room. The new officer unlocked the door, tapped Rico on his shoulder and said, 'Wait in here for a while. It's much better than those cells.'

Rico walked in. He thought the room was empty, but then he saw Karima sitting on the floor in a corner.

'Karima!' Rico shouted.

Karima didn't say anything; she just stood up and walked towards Rico. As she walked towards him, Rico opened his arms to hug her, but she hit him in his left eye with a punch so fast Rico did not see it coming. He saw stars. As he cupped his face in his hands he felt a kick to his ribcage that threw him to the ground. Rico curled up into a ball and Karima sat on him and began pounding his head and back with her fists, shouting, 'You supposed to be my friend, brov. What you been saying about me? What kind of rubbish you been telling the cops, hey? Hey? You supposed to be my friend.'

Rico was so overwhelmed that he couldn't find the energy to speak. He had neither air in his lungs nor space to move. He could not match Karima's kick-boxing, but he also knew she could knock him out if he just stayed down and did nothing. Using all the strength he had, he forced himself to his feet with Karima still going at him, but he managed to stagger into a corner and shout.

'What have I done?'

Karima stood back. 'You know what you've done.' She then delivered a kick to his leg that made him want to go back down, but by sheer will he stayed on his feet.

'Karima – stop, listen. I haven't said anything,' Rico pleaded.

Karima, still in kick-box stance as if waiting to strike, shouted, 'So since when did I convert you to Islam then?'

'I never said that – and you know I wouldn't.'

'And when did I ask you about how to make bombs then?'

'I didn't say that, Karima, either. Honestly.'

'I told you I'm not interested in burning anything up any more.'

'I know. I know. Honestly, I didn't say anything about that stuff.'

They looked at each other. Karima's eyes were red and wet with tears of anger. Rico's eye was purple and already beginning to swell.

'Karima,' said Rico, with one hand covering his eye and the other pointing towards the ceiling. 'Can't you see? Look around you. Cameras are everywhere. This is a set-up. They put us together to see if we would start talking.'

Karima looked up and around at the cameras on the ceiling. Rico continued.

'Why would they put us together? Why wouldn't they come and stop us from fighting?'

Karima looked at the pitiful state that Rico was in – not just at the damage that she had done to him, but at his broken spirit. She then went back to sit in the corner and said, 'I think you're right. I'm sorry, brov. I'm just messed up at the moment. Nothing makes sense.'

Rico looked down at Karima in the corner. To him her spirit looked broken too. He went over and sat next to her, and for a while they both sat in silence until Rico spoke.

'They're watching us.'

'I know,' said Karima.

'All we have to do is tell the truth, right?' said Rico.

'That's right, brov. The truth. That should do the job.'

Chapter 25

Judgement Days

The next day, Rico had another meeting with his lawyer. Karima also had a visit from a lawyer, who had been recommended to her by a local law centre, but Karima and Rico were kept apart until they stood next to each other in court on Monday morning. The court was packed with members of Karima's family, the press and Rico's family, including Lola and Kim. Lola was sitting between her parents, the three of them holding hands.

It was a quick hearing. Rico and Karima confirmed their names, addresses and ages, and their lawyers entered their pleas. Karima pleaded not guilty to all the charges and Rico pleaded not guilty to handling explosives, and not guilty to nine charges of murder. But he did plead guilty to computer hacking. They were both remanded in custody until their appearance in the Crown Court.

Both were detained in the same high-security youth unit. Although they were never allowed to see each other, they were both subject to rule 43, a rule that kept suspected terrorists separated from other prisoners for their own protection. They saw newspaper stories about themselves where their capture was seen as a victory in the war on terror. Journalists were investigating the histories of their families, and they both felt helpless, unable to defend themselves or their relatives from the intrusion. Some newspapers portrayed them as evil, fanatical young people, and to a whole range of extreme groups they were heroes. Karima and Rico thought they were none of these things.

On the day of the Crown Court hearing, Jackson Jones was there to support Rico, but his firm had employed Michael Fieldsman, the country's best-known human rights barrister, to represent him. Before they went into the courtroom, Michael Fieldsman had a meeting with Rico where he explained that he had spoken to his parents, and was dedicated to representing him because he had examined the case and believed that Rico had been exploited. He promised to tell Rico's story as best he could. He also said that he felt this was so important that he would waive his fee.

Michael Fieldsman presented Rico's case with so much passion and attention to detail that it sounded as if he was a witness to it all. He had done a survey of the area and was able to show exactly where the street cameras were. He argued that the reason Speech had restricted their movements when they met was because he was avoiding the street cameras. They were always in camera blind spots. He called Ana as a witness, and she told the court that she did have a birthday just after the date of the explosion, and that her dream was to start a dressmaking business. She had no idea who Speech was, but her birthday was on a couple of social networking sites. When Speech had asked Rico to build the website and then check for his speeding ticket, he was just testing Rico; he wanted to see how good his computer skills were. The car registration number he'd given didn't even exist. Michael Fieldsman summed up his defence of Rico by telling the court that, like Michael Fieldsman himself, Rico was someone who wanted to see justice in the world. He was someone who wanted to do something about injustice. He urged the court to see that it was Rico's idealism that had been exploited, allowing him to be tricked and manipulated, and that he had committed a crime, but he was not a terrorist or a mass murderer.

After all the evidence from both the prosecution and defence had been presented to the court, the jury gave their verdict. Karima was found not guilty of all charges, and released with immediate effect, and Rico was found not guilty of handling explosives, not guilty of nine counts of murder, but guilty of unlawful use of a computer, and unauthorised computer access. He was sentenced to twelve months in youth custody. When he heard the sentence Rico showed no emotion. He was relieved that the court realised that he really wasn't a terrorist, and he accepted that twelve months was much better than a life sentence – but there was nothing to celebrate. He looked around and saw and heard members of his family breathing sighs of relief. His mother nodded her head just a little, his father wiped his forehead with his hand,

and Lola gave a small smile. It was bittersweet. As Rico finished scanning the courtroom it hit home how they were all there because of him. He looked back to his family and as he thought about all the trouble he had caused them his eyes began to fill with tears, but just then two police officers grabbed his arms and he was led out of the court.

Karima went home with her family. Rico went to jail. They transported him from the court in a small cell in a secure van. As they left the court a horde of press photographers ran after the van putting their cameras to the windows, desperate to get an image of him, but as the van gathered speed they were left standing. Rico looked back out of a darkened window to see curious members of the public looking his way. He watched as they got smaller, but then the last person he saw, standing impassively as if he was a passer-by who just happened to be there, was Speech. Rico's heart skipped a beat. He narrowed his eyes and clenched his fists, and then watched as Speech became smaller and smaller, and disappeared. Rico let his anger go, sat down in his mobile prison, and began to think about all the things he would never do again.

Hope and Fear

I was militant and lonely
When my innocence was battered;
There was no one to hold me
When the hope I had was shattered.
My city and my life in flames
All our foundations shaking;
Fake people playing deadly games –
Not fire of my making.

I too have suffered terror
It came to me in person;
I made a drastic error –
Now I must bear the burden,
I was shaken by the horror –
Don't mock my immaturity;
For in my darkest hour –
I was tricked into this tragedy.

This tragedy has broken me,
I struggle to communicate,
I'm trying to hold my sanity –
Their bombs do not discriminate –
This tragedy keeps killing me,
My self-esteem must be rebuilt,
I used to dream of being free –
Now I am filled with fear and guilt.

I must rise up and forward on
And overcome the guilt and fear,
Now my innocence has gone
And I must serve my sentence here;
I too have suffered terror,
And I still dream of being free,
But I promise to do better –
And not let evil conquer me.

Benjamin Zephaniah

Benjamin Zephaniah was born and raised in Handsworth, Birmingham. By the age of fifteen he had gained a reputation as a young poet who was capable of speaking out on local and international issues. His poetry was strongly influenced by the music and poetry of Jamaica and what he called 'street politics'. He is also a musician and was the first person to record with the Wailers after the death of Bob Marley.

As well as writing poetry, novels for teenagers, screenplays and stage plays, he has also written and presented documentaries for television and radio, and he has been awarded sixteen honorary doctorates in recognition of his work. He is now a professor of Poetry and Creative Writing at Brunel University and lives in Lincolnshire. To find out more about Benjamin, go to www.benjaminzephaniah.com or follow him on Twitter: @BZephaniah

F ZEP

WARWICK
LIBRARY
SCHOOL